18

Bolan pre
muzzle ag
cheek

"Captain Makal sends his regards," he said.

Bolan nodded to Sengor, who grabbed two full bags of money. The Executioner leaned down and picked up the wounded man and hurled him through the doorway. Sengor had brought in a canister of gasoline with him, and left it behind when he evacuated, all part of Bolan's plan.

Bolan tore off the cap and splashed the flammable liquid across the remaining money and corpses. He threw the container in the corner, pulled out a disposable lighter and fired it up.

The money-room was an inferno within thirty seconds, but by then, the Executioner was already en route to his next war zone.

MACK BOLAN ®
The Executioner

The Executioner®
Don Pendleton's

AFTERSHOCK

A GOLD EAGLE BOOK FROM
WORLDWIDE®

TORONTO • NEW YORK • LONDON
AMSTERDAM • PARIS • SYDNEY • HAMBURG
STOCKHOLM • ATHENS • TOKYO • MILAN
MADRID • WARSAW • BUDAPEST • AUCKLAND

First edition August 2006
ISBN-13: 978-0-373-64333-2
ISBN-10:   0-373-64333-0

Special thanks and acknowledgment to
Doug Wojtowicz for his contribution to this work.

AFTERSHOCK

Profit is sweet, even if it comes from deception.
—Sophocles, 496–406 B.C.

Make your blood money and enjoy it while you can. The reckoning for your deceptions will be paid off, and I will collect.
—Mack Bolan

To the Red Cross for the lives they've
saved around the world.

Prologue

The Turkish morning sun burned down on the city of Van and the crowded streets full of frightened and shell-shocked citizens. The ceaseless battle between the Turkish military security forces, Jandarma, and the Kongra-Gel terrorists was hottest in the southeastern region where Van was located. Cops were on every corner, and a small command post was set up by the hotel. Officially it was to protect American relief workers, but the soldiers stationed there were more interested in keeping an eye on the foreigners. They were wary of the strangers, realizing that the relief workers, or tourists in the same hotel, could be in league with the Kongra-Gel revolutionary front.

Boz Arcuri looked both ways before he got out of the Peugeot. The 9 mm Llama in his waistband was uncocked, but he could thumb the hammer back in a heartbeat and put all nine shots from the sleek handgun into anyone who challenged him.

Still, his black, scraggly beard was trimmed, and his clothes were neat and clean, despite their loose fit, allowing his shirt to cover the trim outline of his pistol. He frowned. The hotel he'd parked in front of wasn't one of the best in Van, but it was loaded with relief workers, and frugal tourists from a dozen nations. The presence of the military so close by provided the foreigners with a false sense of security.

Westerners were comforted by the sight of soldiers, regardless of how truly effective they were in protecting them. Arcuri thought of the time he'd gone to the United States, setting up a heroin deal with a New York Mob boss. Since that dark September day, it wasn't unusual to find men and women carrying assault rifles, but to the Kongra-Gel lieutenant's experienced eye, he realized that those National Guardsmen were holding empty weapons, no magazines in place. A calculating enough assassin could kill a half-dozen of the armed guards and get a supply of pristine, unfired automatic weapons to unleash a wave of devastation among them.

Though the Turkish army troops had magazines in their weapons, they suffered from the conceit of many Middle Eastern men. They refused to use their shoulder stocks, and many of them had folded their metal stocks, or sawn off the wooden units, making their rifles ineffective and useless farther than twenty feet out.

Arcuri felt secure as he walked away from the truck. Its covered bed was stuffed with four thousand pounds of mixed fertilizer, plastic explosives and small arms shells that had been damaged in transport, or didn't fit Kongra-Gel's arsenal of weapons, all packed in a flat cake that was neatly concealed by a simple tarpaulin. Mixing in the bullets was a stroke of genius. It disposed of useless ammunition and created simple, effective shrapnel that would only add to the mayhem.

The goal of the bombing wasn't to strike any specific blow, but the detonation would provide a thundering distraction for the Turkish rebels' true goals.

The Multinational Organization Relief Effort for Southeast Turkey—MOREST—had a storehouse of drugs, including painkillers, that Kongra-Gel could steal and sell for millions of dollars, keeping a small supply for their own forces to continue the fight against the western-poisoned government. Arcuri grinned and walked. A bomb going off at the hotel would draw the relief workers and guards hired to protect the medical supplies to the scene of the bombing. It would leave only a minor skeleton crew on hand to protect the golden egg that Kagan Trug wanted.

After that, it would be easy to swoop in. The Kongra-Gel team was organized, had its trucks in position and only needed one thing to make the heist come off cleanly.

Arcuri looked around. The lawman standing on the street corner, pistol in his belt holster, dark eyes scanning the faces of passersby, had only noticed Arcuri in passing. The rebel Turk pulled his Llama from under his shirt as he'd gotten within an arm's length. A woman's scream alerted the cop that there was danger, but it was too late for him. Arcuri pulled the trigger, emptying nine rounds into the doomed policeman's skull. As the cop fell, the terrorist turned his attention back to the military forces by the hotel. They heard the shooting and grabbed their rifles, racing in a throng toward the sound of gunfire.

When the main pack of Turkish soldiers reached his Peugeot, Arcuri grinned and pressed the button on the radio detonator in his pocket. Even five blocks down the street from ground zero, the Kongra-Gel lieutenant was knocked off his feet by the blast wave. The fireball extended three hundred feet in every direction.

Anyone inside that dome of flame and pressure was instantly vaporized. Even the protection of walls and windows were useless as ripples of explosive force shattered brick and turned glass into clouds of high-velocity shrapnel. Arcuri crawled to the cover of a parked car and watched in awe as the hotel shook violently.

The vehicle he huddled against rattled as debris rained atop it. A moment later, the half of the hotel facing the pickup truck expelled jets of dust and smoke from its shattered windows, and slid to the ground in a choking cloud of gray.

Arcuri struggled to his feet. The world had been flipped

onto its ear, and wails of pain and terror erupted from the thick blanket of swirling debris that grew, crawling ominously toward Arcuri. The Turk grinned and gave the cloud a small salute, racing off down the street. One cop fired three shots after him, a bullet clipping the sleeve of his jacket, but another Turkish officer dragged the gunman toward the carnage, the act of saving lives more important than bringing in the madman, for the time being.

Arcuri raced to freedom, knowing his brothers would be hard at work, looting the warehouse.

IN THE KANDILLI Observatory and Earthquake Research Institute, scientists registered the tremor in downtown Van. It drew attention, but not as much as it should have, as the radio and television displayed the news of the destruction of the hotel and the deaths of hundreds.

Vigo Pepis, however, was watching the sensors. The vibrations they picked up from the explosion in Van lasted longer. He tried to tell his coworkers about the aberration, but he was brushed off, told that the collapse of the building would have contributed to the odd readings.

Pepis looked at the graph. He could see on the scope the rhythm of the tremors caused by the explosion, and moments later, the collapse of the hotel. There was a definite beat, but a background vibration wave had started a moment before the detonation, hidden by the spike in pressure waves caused by the explosion. Pepis wished he could have seen the scope of the tremor. He was good at predicting earthquakes, but he needed clean, uninterrupted data. The bombing in Van had hit at just the wrong moment for Pepis to tell if the minor quake was a prelude to something worse, an initial breech of pent-up energy between fault lines crushed against each other, or just standard shakes as the earth flexed as part of its natural shifting.

The graph suddenly began going again.

"Vigo! Oh my God… Look!" Taira shouted.

Pepis glanced up momentarily from the graph to see the damaged hotel shake again. Another section collapsed, and he snapped back to the graph. The plates flexed against each other. Something had happened. He was certain a major earthquake was building up. The collapse of another section of building masked more of the seismic vibrations in Van, but nearby sensors, twenty and fifty miles from the city center, picked up sympathetic tremors.

"It's going to be a disaster," Pepis muttered weakly.

"What are you talking about?" Taira asked. "It already is! I can't imagine how many people are trapped under the rubble."

Pepis's lips drew into a tight and bloodless line.

"It's going to get worse," he whispered. "Much, much worse."

The Executioner whipped around and leveled the AK-47 at the midsection of the armed thug, stitching him from crotch to sternum with a line of .30-caliber holes. Belly blasted into a gory crater, the gunman's corpse toppled off the back of the pickup truck and Mack Bolan turned to slide through the rear window of its cab. Gunfire chased after him, but bullets deflected off the sides of the truck.

The driver, his skull dented by a point-blank burst, blocked the Executioner from getting fully inside the pickup. The vehicle rolled out of control toward the gate of the Kongra-Gel facility. Bolan let the emptied AK drop to the pickup's bed so he could use both hands to steer for the center of the wooden doors. He pushed hard against the corpse's knee, using the lifeless leg to stomp on the accelerator. The truck raced faster and Bolan held on, white-knuckled, to the steering wheel.

The front fender met the barrier, and two tons of steel defeated the heavy wooden doors. The impact jolted Bolan farther into the cab, and he twisted like a serpent. His legs slipped through the rear window and he dropped into the leg well of the shotgun seat as a fresh storm of autofire tore through the cab. The lifeless driver jerked spasmodically as 7.62 mm ComBloc rounds burst gory exit wounds from his chest, the heavy-caliber bullets smashing the steering column into useless metal and plastic.

The Executioner realized that he didn't have much longer and pried open the passenger-side door. His long legs extended fully, like steel coil springs, and launched him out the door and into a thicket of bushes as the bullet-riddled pickup truck tumbled onward. The Toyota's grille collapsed as it hit a tree. Where the unbraced doors had proved vulnerable, the old, deep-rooted tree was an immovable object. The driver's corpse vaulted through the windshield and slid down the hood, leaving a gory smear.

Bolan drew his Jericho pistol and checked its load, then headed deeper into the roadside foliage. The spectacular crash of the pickup truck had bought him a few precious moments to reach cover, and he took it. The Jericho was a stand-in for Bolan's usual Desert Eagle. Getting across the border hadn't given the soldier much of an opportunity to shop for weapons, but he was able to get the gun, in .40 S&W, and several hundred rounds of ammunition for it. Even though it wasn't the full-sized .44 Magnum he was used to, the "baby Desert Eagle" would give any pursuer pause, and give the soldier an opportunity to acquire a longer range weapon. And if he couldn't, he'd improvise.

The soft probe of the Kongra-Gel camp had proved disastrous, an example of bad luck as a guard had been able to get off a shot before the Executioner could silence him. Bolan hadn't had an opportunity to lay the explosives he needed to destroy the training area and the barracks of the Turkish narcoterrorists responsible for the deaths of almost two hundred American and British relief workers, and more than three hundred Turkish citizens in the Van bombing.

He'd only just finished a mission in Azerbaijan, taking out a ring of arms smugglers when he'd heard about the brutal attack in Turkey. Bolan was too late to protect the victims of the Kongra-Gel, an amalgamation of various Turkish Communist insurgent groups. However, a quick conference call with Aaron Kurtzman and Hal Brognola at Stony Man Farm had indicated that the hellish murders were simply a diversion to cover the theft of millions of dollars' worth of relief supplies, including medications and painkillers meant for the displaced refugees from the incessant civil war waged by these very thieves.

It was a small step up from heroin and opium dealing to flooding the black market with drugs meant for their own countrymen. Bolan hoped to find the missing drugs and supplies before the savage thugs sold them off, and perhaps get them back to work in helping the Turkish refugees. It was the least that the Executioner could do to further the cause of the MOREST lifesavers.

They had been slain in the course of their work to make the world a better place.

Bolan wasn't going to let their murderers profit from their savagery.

The Executioner paused at the base of the hill and spotted a half-dozen gunmen making their way around the bend. They were out of breath from taking the road and had slowed down, eyes wide and wary against the lethal black shadow who had torn through twenty of their brethren. Rifle muzzles swept the roadside, bodies reacting to the rustle of leaves in the breeze. Bolan frowned as he recognized that they were maintaining their calm. They were alert, not panicked, and weren't going to waste their ammunition on an uncertain target.

Bolan was running low on major gear and supplies. It had taken him six hours to smuggle himself into Turkey, pick up a couple of handguns along with a smattering of plastic explosives and a battle harness. He'd used up his grenades in a savage firefight against the Azerbaijani gunrunners. That was why he'd made the soft probe against the Kongra-Gel training camp, to scrounge for supplies and intel, and to give the organization's leadership something to sweat over.

The Executioner knew he'd come in behind the eight ball,

but he wouldn't allow that to hobble him. He wadded up a cube of C-4 and rolled it in a stash of stones and pebbles that an ant colony had built up to secure their nest. The insects fled from the slowly rolling ball as their rocky pile was imbedded into the soft, pliant explosive. Bolan pressed a pencil-sized radio detonator into the round, rocky blob, and let fly with the improvised grenade.

The Turkish rebels spotted Bolan's movement and one of them fired a short burst toward the tree that he'd been huddled against. Bark splintered as the incongruous bomb landed in the midst of the gunmen. They looked down at it, an ersatz, gray candy apple with a blinking stick poking out of it. Because it didn't look like a grenade, they were confused by its presence. More of the riflemen opened up, but the Executioner thumbed the firing stud on his detonator.

The explosion tore one of the terrorist thugs in two, a sheet of force pushing a guillotine of rock through the centerline of his body. Another man died as a quarter-inch-wide pebble tore through his right eye and whipped through his brain like a bullet. Another one wailed as his left arm was stripped of flesh all the way to the bone.

It wasn't much of an advantage, but it would have to do, Bolan figured as he burst from cover, the big Jericho bucking in his fist. The Executioner's first shot caught a Turkish terrorist on the bridge of his nose and blew a flap of scalp and skull off the back of his head. A second killer leaped wildly for the cover of a ditch, but Bolan caught him with a bullet through his left thigh. Muscle and bone were mangled by the heavy-caliber slug and the rifleman disappeared out of sight, screaming in pain.

The last able gunman, his right side bloodied, uniform torn by shrapnel, snarled angrily and milked the trigger of his AK-47 in an effort to avenge his injuries. Bolan pivoted and leaped forward beneath the stream of autofire, pumping out four shots. One missed, sailing into the distance over the wounded Turk's shoulder, but his other shots connected with the Kongra-Gel killer's torso, zipping him from throat to groin.

The wounded rifleman struggled to grab his AK's pistol grip with his left hand, determined to protect himself when Bolan somersaulted onto the road. The Executioner lashed out with one of his stovepipe legs, his heel catching the rifle. The kick launched the weapon into the roadside ditch, and Bolan leveled his Jericho at the Turk.

"Don't even try it," the soldier warned.

The Kongra-Gel fighter froze as he looked down the hole in the end of the massive pistol.

"Run away," Bolan said, jerking the muzzle slightly. "Live to fight another day."

The Turk looked over his shoulder, then back at the huge handgun aimed at him.

If he didn't understand Bolan's words, he at least understood the intent of his gestures. The Turk cradled his mangled arm and raced off down the road, not looking back.

Bolan scrambled to his feet and dumped the partially empty magazine, reloading with a fully loaded stick of twelve more hollowpoint rounds. He pocketed the half-empty clip and slowly advanced toward the gunman cowering in the ditch.

A burst of automatic fire was the Executioner's welcome, the swarm of bullets burning hotly, too close for comfort. Bolan dived to the bottom of the ditch and punched two more rounds into the hobbled rifleman before the Turk could adjust his aim. The rounds were fatal, one plowing through the gunman's groin and smashing his spine, the second tearing into his heart.

The Executioner holstered his pistol and picked up the AK-47 and the dead man's spare ammo. He walked into the road and pulled more ammunition off the other dead men, inspecting the banana-shaped magazines for damage before loading them into a borrowed bandolier bag. Five of the clips had been mangled by the explosion, and nothing could be retrieved from the torn corpse of Bolan's first target.

It didn't matter. He had twelve full magazines, and five more half-filled boxes that he could load to make it an even fifteen sticks for the confiscated AK. The rounds of rifle ammunition would be enough to keep Bolan solvent in his war against the Kongra-Gel and the recovery of the missing supplies.

Two-dozen dead, and one survivor who would take a message to the group's leadership.

They were no longer the prime predators in southeast Turkey.

The Executioner had arrived, and there was going to be hell to pay. He was going to shake the country and see what rattled loose in the aftermath.

2

Catherine Abood grunted as she was hurled against the jeep's fender by the Jandarma goon. She put the back of her hand to her mouth, and wasn't surprised by the bright red seeping across her skin when it came away. She took a deep breath and spit out blood, and glared, dark eyed, at the thugs.

She'd taken pictures of what these creeps had done to a teen-aged boy they suspected of knowing members of the Kongra-Gel. Her camera was torn open, its film exposed while another of the rifle-toting thugs crushed her remaining canisters of film.

"We can't allow this to fall into the wrong hands," the Jandarma commander, Captain Yuli Makal, told her.

"Since when do you care what the West thinks?" Abood asked as Makal snatched her wrist and pulled her close.

Abood realized that antagonizing these thugs was the worst possible choice she could have made, but her father had raised her to be an independent woman. He'd taught her how to shoot, how to fight, how to protect herself, and encouraged her to break the mold of a demure, soft-spoken Arab woman. She was born and raised an American, a fourth generation New Englander, but by the time she was fourteen, she'd seen most of the world. From Kudu hunts in South Africa to ski-ing in Switzerland, she'd avoided a sheltered life.

Makal smirked as he felt her waist, then pushed open her photographer's vest. "You have a gun, young lady."

"I have a permit for it," Abood stated. Her cheek and lips felt thick, probably swollen from Makal's punch. "Your government wants me to have it."

Makal looked at the 9 mm Beretta Compact, admiring its balance and feel. "But you have the protection of the Jandarma, my sweet thing," he said.

Makal's smile split his homely face. His head rested on his broad shoulders like a fireplug topped with curly, thick, greasy hair. A bushy mustache flapped over that yellowed smile. They were eye to eye, and though Abood was tall, at five feet, seven inches, it only pointed out how her willowy frame made her stand out among the Turkish people.

Though her Syrian blood had given her an olive complexion, it was not as sun-and-wind darkened as the natives. She was relatively pale, and her long black hair flowed like silk. Her smile would have been much whiter had it not been for the blood smeared across her teeth from Makal's punch.

"Who gave you such a fine gun, my sweetie?"

"My father," Abood answered, her eyes narrowed. She struggled, but she was wary of the trio of riflemen watching her intently. She knew how to fight, how to shoot, how to protect herself, but she also knew that pulling a pistol against an armed force of semiofficial vigilantes patrolling the Turkish countryside would be tantamount to suicide. She bided her time.

"Ah," Makal said. "Did you add the pretty sights and grips, or did he?"

Abood glowered. Makal's fist squeezed her wrist, and she felt the bones in her forearm start to rub together. He would keep grinding them until her arm was crippled or he'd gotten an answer. "He did. But that's why I like it so much."

"It's worth money, then," Makal said as he stuffed the handgun behind the buckle of his belt. Abood resisted the urge to warn him against shooting his dick off, partially because the pistol's safety was on, and pissing him off would only make things worse for her. Makal rubbed a hard, callused hand across her smooth cheek. "As are you, no?"

"My magazine does not make deals with terrorists," Abood answered.

The caress turned into a hard slap, and Abood sprawled across the hood of the jeep.

"We are the law in this country," Makal snarled. "We are justice."

Abood glared. Her ingrained response had landed her in trouble. Makal adjusted his belt and placed his rough hand over the crotch of his pants. "Usually, we're not as well compensated for our efforts...."

Abood looked at the trio of riflemen watching her. Their weapons were aimed at the ground and wicked smirks danced across their features. One slung his weapon and began to undo his belt.

"That is Etter," Makal explained. "He's our warm-up for these things."

"Warm-up?" Abood repeated, a chill flashing across her skin like lightning.

"Some women are a bit...tight," Makal continued. "He loosens things up."

Etter chuckled, sounding like a mentally deranged cartoon character as he opened his trousers. While the Turk wasn't a big man, only a couple of inches taller than Abood, he was freakishly endowed. Abood gritted her teeth, knowing she'd better think of something before these bastards had their way with her. Unfortunately, the two men who had been destroying her equipment finished and flanked the group.

"We got everything," one soldier said.

"Almost everything," the other said with a chuckle as he looked at Abood.

Makal nodded. "Hold her."

The two newcomers slung their rifles, and Abood acted instantly. She kicked Makal in the stomach, the toe of her boot knocking the Beretta to the road and forcing the Jandarma captain to stumble backward. Etter paused, then lunged forward, one beefy hand grabbing at her blouse, but Abood reacted fluidly. The heel of her palm caught the Turk between his lip and nose and snapped Etter's head back. Unbalanced, his legs constrained by his half-fallen pants, the Turk flopped to the road.

She snaked her arm free from one of the soldiers who grabbed at her, but the other latched on to the arm that had knocked their partner onto his rear. Abood twisted and punched the goon in the sternum, but even driving the wind out of the Jandarma soldier didn't relax the rapist's grip.

"Fuck you!" Abood screamed, letting the clingy Turk get a face full of her loudest yell. It distracted him from her foot snaking around his ankle and she folded her arm abruptly. The point of her elbow struck the man in the breastbone and he fell to one side, dragging her down with him.

"Whore!" the other two would-be rapists growled, and they rushed forward. Abood twisted and pulled her wrestling partner against her, a shield that took the first brutal swings of their rifle stocks.

It wasn't much, and they were going to make her pay for her resistance, but she was not going to surrender meekly. She was going to go down fighting.

"Drop the rifles!" a voice suddenly shouted.

The gunmen paused. Abood thrashed free, clawing out into the open.

"They're trying to rape me!" she shouted.

"Nobody move!" the newcomer shouted. Abood's eyes cleared and she spotted the man. He was tall, well built, wearing a dark, body-conforming outfit that showed off his rippling arms and chest where his torso peeked through a pouch-laden harness. He held an AK-47 in his hands, and his gaze was hard and stern.

Etter scooped up his rifle and triggered it, but holding the weapon one-handed, his initial burst missed. That was all the man in black needed to explode into action. A fiery lance of gunfire stabbed into the half-dressed rapist, heavy-caliber slugs punching through his head and neck. Explosions of gore and the rattle of automatic weapons spurred the remaining riflemen into action, and they went for their own guns. The tall man took three steps, seeming to weave ahead of the Turkish thugs as they tried to bear down on him. The mysterious avenger's weapon ripped out another stream of slugs and decapitated one of the riflemen.

Abood didn't know who he was, but this man was quick and skillful. Still, he was outnumbered, and she saw her Beretta lying in the gravel. She lunged for the pistol and almost got it when Makal's weight slammed into her, a big hand clawing at her forearm. Abood turned and showed her own claws, fingers raking across the Turk's left eye. Blood squirted over her fingers as she dug in, and the Jandarma commander's fetid breath washed over her, accompanied by a wail of pain. Abood punched hard, tagging him in the nose. Cartilage collapsed under the impact, and Makal squirmed to one side, rolling into a roadside ditch.

Abood vaulted forward and grabbed her handgun.

"Get out of the way!" the man shouted as Abood swung toward the Turkish captain, but Abood triggered two shots. Makal twitched as a 9 mm hollowpoint round ripped through his arm. The fireplug-headed goon raced into the woods.

Abood whirled and the tall man lowered his rifle.

"Are you hurt?" he asked.

Abood brushed her mouth. One corner was swollen and tender to the touch, but the blood flow had stopped. "It'll be awhile before I play the saxophone again…."

The man regarded her. Though his skin was tanned a deep, rich brown by exposure to the sun, he was most decidedly not a Semitic man. Too tall, too classically Anglo. Abood couldn't exactly place him by look, and thought if he wore sunglasses to conceal those cold, ice-blue eyes, he could have fit in anywhere from a Marrakech market to a Hong Kong casino.

"It was a joke," Abood said, her words slurred slightly as right side of her mouth reacted numbly to her words.

"They didn't do any permanent damage?" he said.

"No. I'll be okay," Abood answered. She looked down and saw blood spattered across her torn blouse. "Most of this blood isn't mine."

He extended a hand to her. "Name's Brandon Stone," Mack Bolan said, using a cover identity.

"Catherine Abood, *Newsworld* magazine," she introduced herself. "Everyone calls me Cat."

A hint of recognition showed in Bolan's face. "You did an article on a white slavery ring operating in Lebanon last year," Bolan said.

"Yup. Would I know of your work anywhere, Mr.—"

"Colonel," Bolan corrected.

"Colonel Stone?" Abood asked.

Bolan shook his head. "Nothing I could confirm or deny."

Abood nodded. "One of those kinds of guys."

"Afraid so," Bolan replied. "We'd better get out of here."

Abood nodded, and she stepped over to the Jandarma soldier who lay stunned beside her Jeep. She picked up his rifle and grabbed a couple of magazines, stuffing them into the voluminous pockets of her vest. She stuffed her Beretta back into its holster after reloading it. "They took out my equipment."

Bolan looked around. "What did you witness?"

"They skinned a teenaged boy and lit his hair on fire," Abood answered softly. She was disgusted at how easily she could repeat the events. "They saw me and chased me down."

"You're lucky they didn't just kill you," Bolan stated as he headed toward one of the jeeps. "Who were they? Kongra-Gel?"

"Jandarma," Abood answered.

Bolan stopped and frowned, his hard eyes suddenly troubled. His gaze refocused. "They're official in this province?"

"Official enough that the government never prosecutes them for excessive force if there's not enough evidence," Abood said.

"Like photographs taken by a foreign journalist," Bolan suggested.

"Right," Abood replied. "After that, it would be my word against theirs…if I survived."

"The government wouldn't have believed your accusations without photographic evidence," Bolan stated. "I know these types of groups."

"Intimately?" Abood asked, slightly nervous.

"We've butted heads more than a couple times," Bolan said.

"Yeah," Abood agreed with a sigh. "You look like a tough customer, but you are definitely not one of these scumbags."

Abood chewed over his words for a moment. "You're from New England too. Lost most of the accent, but I can still hear it."

"Massachusetts," Bolan replied. "New Hampshire?"

Abood nodded. "Yup."

"We'll have old-home week on the way out of here," Bolan told her. "Right now, I want to get you to safety."

"I can handle myself," Abood said, defiant.

"I'm sure you can," the Executioner answered, no condescension in his tone. "But you were in over your head. Get in the jeep."

"Who've you been butting heads with over here?" Abood asked, climbing into the shotgun seat.

"Sorry, I don't have time for interviews," Bolan stated as he started up the vehicle and tromped on the gas.

"It's not an interview. I just want to know what's gotten you spooked."

Bolan sighed as he performed a hairpin turn. "Kongra-Gel."

"The bombing in Van," Abood said. "I was investigating that when I ran afoul of the storm troopers back there."

Bolan looked in the side mirror.

Abood looked over her shoulder and saw what had caught the big man's attention. "Shit."

"Yeah. The one you winged just waved down some buddies," Bolan said as he looked at the trucks in the distance. He gunned the engine, squeezing more speed out of the vehicle.

"No wonder you were in a hurry," Abood said, settling down in her seat.

"Hang on tight. This is going to get a little bumpy," Mack Bolan told the reporter as he swerved around a bend in the road.

3

Kandilli Observatory and Earthquake Research Institute

"Sir, I believe we're heading toward a major disaster. We have to let the media know," Vigo Pepis said to Kan Bursa, the director of the observatory.

"Nothing is clear on the graph, though," Bursa answered, concern coloring his features. "And none of the other seismologists have been able to confirm on their readings."

"I know. The background tremors caused by the bombing and the collapse of the buildings in the area have masked any readings in the city," Pepis explained. "But just take a look at what I've recorded. Outlying sensor reports seem weaker, meaning that the epicenter is going to be right beneath Van itself."

"There's nothing to reinforce that fact," Bursa replied.

"That's because of Lake Van," Pepis explained. "Sensors can't pick up anything because we couldn't place the ground sensors in a conventional perimeter. With the closest western land more than one hundred miles away, we're not going to get properly effective readings."

"How about the data we're receiving from NASA?" Bursa asked.

"The satellite placed in orbit over Turkey is currently being worked on by their shuttle," Pepis stated. "It'll be another eighteen hours before we have a current observation of thermal patterns. However, there was a lava buildup on the infrared scans of the area before the scope went down."

Bursa chewed his lower lip. "I'll put out a warning, but Van is already under martial law. The military, police and Jandarma are on the hunt for the bastards who attacked the relief workers."

"Then we have an infrastructure already in place," Pepis said. "That's good."

"They're hunting for terrorists," Bursa explained. "If something does hit, they're going to be spread doubly thin."

"You don't think that the Kongras would strike in the aftermath of an earthquake, do you?" Pepis asked.

"They might not," Bursa said. "Usually, when we've had big earthquakes in the past, we've been able to rely on a general ceasefire to keep everyone in line."

"But they already hit the medical supply warehouse," Pepis stated.

"And relief workers," Bursa added. "I'll talk to the minister of defense and the minister of the interior, but right now, the earth isn't the only threat we have to deal with. I'm sorry, Vigo."

Pepis took a deep breath and let it out slowly. He nodded in quiet acceptance.

"How bad do you think it will be?" Bursa asked.

"Huge," Pepis answered softly. "At least a 7.0."

"You think it'll be worse."

Pepis nodded, almost spasmodically.

"I don't have to remind anyone in the ministry of the interior that a 7.2 earthquake killed thousands of people a few years back," Bursa grumbled, watching his best seismologist's reaction.

"I'm praying it's not going to be that bad," Pepis said. "But sometimes your prayers don't get answered."

Bursa looked at the map of Van. "Bombings, civil war...and now an earthquake. If that city ever needed heroes, it needs them now."

THE EXECUTIONER'S BATTLE instincts were on alert. He saw the Jandarma jeeps racing to keep up with his vehicle, and even though they were loaded down with armed riflemen, they kept a decent pace with the much lighter jeep he was steering. Something else kept him on edge, though. Bolan didn't believe in psychic phenomena, but he had enough experiences with subconsciously detected threat cues to realize that there were senses many people possessed that provided them with early warnings.

Bolan had survived years of war against Animal Man simply because he'd managed to make his subconscious observations a part of his conscious thought. A bulge here, scuffed dirt there, the whisper of a foot across blades of grass or even the whiff of drying blood on a blade were all noticed by his intuitive bubble of early warnings. It wasn't a sixth sense per se, but his mind processing all the data brought before it by his other five senses.

Something was nagging at him, and even as he twisted the jeep around another bend, his mind sought what made him uneasy.

Bolan's soft probe, only an hour ago, had been interrupted because the sentry who had raised the alarm had been on his way to see why the guard dogs in their kennels were on edge and barking. Bolan had slipped into the training camp and made an effort to avoid the dogs, staying upwind of them and keeping out of their finely honed sense of smell. When he moved, he moved with the crescendo of background noise and walking feet so as not to tip off the guard dogs' acute hearing.

So what had set the animals off?

Bolan heard Abood gasp and he yanked on the hand brake, spinning the jeep into a 180-degree turn. Another group of vehicles was racing along the hillside, and Bolan recognized them. They were from the motor pool at the Kongra-Gel camp, and they were joining the merry chase. All this took a heartbeat. The soldier released his handbrake and the jeep raced toward the onrushing Jandarma hunters.

"Who's that?" Abood asked quickly.

"Kongra-Gel," Bolan answered abruptly. "They're after me."

Abood shook her head and gripped her confiscated AK-47. "You make friends everywhere you go?"

"Yeah. Some of them don't even try to kill me," Bolan said. He glanced at the side mirror and caught sight of the Kongra-Gel hunters pushing their vehicles off their road and racing down the scrub-clotted slope to get even with their quarry.

Rifle fire opened up, spraying between the two parties of hunters as they recognized each other. Bolan glanced back as the Kongra-Gel cadre tore past the turning Jandarma pursuit team, their AKs spraying the slowed vehicles. The Turkish security force drivers struggled to keep them in the chase and the crews of their jeeps opened fire on the Kongra-Gel terrorists.

Bolan swerved and plunged his own vehicle off the road, knobby tires slipping on crushed bushes and loose shale, but he steered into the direction of any drift. In a few seconds, Bolan swung his jeep onto a lower road, hooked a hard right and tore down the snaking path through the forest. Automatic fire chattered, but it was wide of the target. Trying to get accuracy out of a moving vehicle, hitting another moving vehicle, was beyond the marksmanship skills of most untrained gunners.

The cut down the side of the hill had bought the Executioner and Abood a ten-second lead, keeping them ahead of the mayhem, but the jeep felt sluggish. Bolan scanned both side mirrors and saw that the right rear tire was at an odd angle. The vehicular gymnastics and off-road racing had twisted the axle and bled some speed. The tough little jeep would keep rolling, but it kept Bolan from reaching top speed, and that would be enough to allow the heavier pursuit vehicles to catch up.

"I wrecked the suspension," Bolan announced. "We're not going to be able to outrace the Jandarmas or the Kongras."

Abood twisted in her seat and looked back down the road. "I caught a glimpse of a front bumper."

Bolan tromped the gas, but the accelerator wasn't giving him more speed. "I'm going to have to slow them down."

Abood looped the sling of her rifle around her shoulders and extended its folding stock. She pressed it tightly and got a good cheek weld. "Just keep driving."

Bolan nodded and hit a straightaway on the road. As the enemy rounded the bend, Abood cut loose with her rifle. Brass rained in the Executioner's hair and one hot casing landed between his skintight top and his battle harness. It was hot, searing his skin, but the fabric of his blacksuit would prevent any permanent damage. A swift glance in the side mirror told him that the lead jeep had turned violently to avoid the stream of automatic fire.

"Thanks for keeping the jeep steady," Abood said. "I still didn't take them out."

"Slowed them down," Bolan told her. "Good shooting."

"My dad's a gun writer," Abood explained as she reloaded her rifle. "He even let me play with some of the law-enforcement-only toys he got to review."

Bolan nodded. "Keep up the good work."

The soldier swung around another curve and hit the brakes. Abood glanced back and Bolan grabbed his rifle. She saw the headlights of a large truck racing toward them on the road.

"Abandon ship," he ordered. "Don't know who they are, but they just cut us off."

Bolan and Abood raced away from the jeep and into the trees. A couple of jeeps rounded the curve too quickly and rear-ended their abandoned vehicle, smashing it between their fenders. The truck slammed into the other end of the jeep and threw the other two aside.

Jandarma gunmen clambered out of the back of the transport truck, and Bolan cursed as he saw a contingent racing into the woods after them while the others rushed to deal with the Kongra-Gel pursuit team. The road erupted with automatic fire between the warring parties, the Jandarma thugs charged through the grove of trees.

"Keep running," Bolan said to Abood.

Bolan stopped and dropped to one knee. He fired two bursts, catching the two frontmost pursuers in the chest, stitching them with heavy-caliber slugs. As the paramilitary Turks dropped to the ground, as if they'd struck an invisible wall, their partners scattered and took cover behind tree trunks.

Abood reached the cover of a tree and braced herself across an exposed root, one-and-a-half feet high. She pointed her rifle and ripped off a short blast of autofire at a goon behind cover. Bolan wasn't certain if she made a hit, but that wasn't his concern as he caught up with her. "Keep moving."

Abood nodded and got up as the Executioner paused at the trunk, flicked the selector switch to semiauto and put the front sight on the head of an adventurous Jandarma rifleman who had broken cover. Bolan stroked the trigger and the AK-47 punched a bullet through the gunner's upper chest. The Executioner noted how far off the sights were from the results of his shot, and took the break in the Jandarma pursuit to continue after Abood.

After two more minutes of running, Bolan and Abood cut

southwest toward Van, passing a stream and disappearing into the forest on the other side of the water. After five minutes, Bolan stopped so that Abood could catch her breath. The pair rested behind a copse of bushes.

Bolan breathed slowly and evenly to recover his breath while Abood gulped down air.

"You all right?" he asked.

"Yeah. Just not in as good shape as I'd like," Abood answered. "Then again, I'm not usually running for my life with fifty pounds of rifle and ammunition."

"Sorry about that," Bolan replied.

The woman shrugged. "You're the reason I'm still alive to bitch about it, Stone."

The soldier smiled. "Glad you could keep it all in perspective."

"It's a talent," Abood answered. "So what's the plan?"

Bolan pulled a laminated map from a pocket of his blacksuit. "Judging by how far we've come and the direction we've taken, Van should be a forty-five-minute walk." He pointed. "That way."

"You're going to need clothes," Abood mentioned. "Unless you don't mind sticking out like a NATO Dense Pack."

"I've got a stash in a roadside ditch, about a forty-minute walk from here," Bolan said.

"Always prepared?" Abood asked.

Bolan nodded. "A friend of mine once referred to me as the original hard-core Boy Scout."

Abood sighed and rolled her eyes. "Just goes to show. I joined the Girl Scouts, but they would never give me a merit badge for marksmanship."

Bolan chuckled. "It's a bit late for that now. Come on, before the Jandarma expands its search for us."

"And what about the Kongra-Gel?" Abood asked. "I take it you have unfinished business here."

"Very observant," Bolan replied. "Once I drop you off somewhere safe, I'll get back to what I was doing. Don't worry about me."

"Don't worry about me, either. This is about the missing drugs, right?" Abood asked. "Listen. I know people. My dad associated with a lot of folks, SEALs, federal cops, all kinds of folks who go into dark places. I don't know what organization you're with, but I do have a feeling that you're more than just some spook busting Turkish Commies."

Bolan remained silent.

"First, you broke cover and started a fight with the Jandarma to protect me, someone you don't know. Second, you expressed some concern when it looked like you could have killed official people, but once you remembered what the Jandarma was, you didn't let it bother you. Third, your plans include making sure I'm safe and secure before you continue your mission," Abood said. "You're not some macho man. You actually care about what you're doing, and there's a lot of lines you're not willing to cross to get it done."

Bolan shrugged. "Or I just could be a sucker for a pretty face."

Abood smiled. "I've been on the same case. If you promise to bring me along to cover the story…"

"There's no story," Bolan explained. "Not with me."

"Then I'm not going to tell you what I know," Abood said defiantly.

"I can live with that," Bolan answered, and he started walking.

Abood jogged to catch up with him. "You can live with that?"

"I have my own ways to get information," Bolan explained.

"Even if the drugs are going to be shipped out to Erzurum tonight?" Abood asked.

Bolan paused. "I know I'm up against a deadline. I also know I'm not going to risk you underfoot, no matter how good a shot you are."

Abood grumbled. "And if those drugs end up on the black market, or destroyed, how many thousands are going to suffer?"

Bolan stopped, his jaw set firmly.

"You're willing to risk your own life to save those people, fighting against the Kongra-Gel all by yourself. But are you willing to risk thousands of refugees if you fail?" Abood asked. "What's one life more in the fray?"

Bolan regarded her coldly. "What's one more life?"

Abood stepped back, stunned by Bolan's voice.

"What's one more life? Plenty. I've lost enough friends and allies over the years. Far too many buddies, too many bystanders. You mentioned that I'm someone who cares about what I'm doing, and that I have lines I won't cross," Bolan said. "You're right. And watching another person die because they got in over their heads is something I refuse to do."

Abood frowned. "But—"

"I know you're used to risking your life, but you do it to get stories. I stay out of the limelight. If you want to save lives, then you tell me what I have to do to keep those drugs from getting out of Van," Bolan told her. "Unless you're willing to risk thousands of people for your own little byline."

"Stone, wait…."

Bolan started walking again. "You've got forty minutes to make your choice. If you haven't made a decision by the time I get to my stash of clothes, I'm walking one way and you're taking a hike. You've got guns. You look after your own safety."

Abood fell silent.

Bolan knew that his decision wasn't appreciated, but he also had his duty. He was as much a defender of lives as an avenger of victims. When it came down to it, anything he could do to deny the Reaper another soul was gravy. If he had to be tough, then so be it.

Better that they lived resenting his rough manner than they died because he was too polite to say what needed to be said.

4

Cat Abood checked her watch. They reached Colonel Stone's stash of backup supplies a good four minutes early, but then, she knew that Stone hadn't counted on walking at a pace to escape his frustration. She looked at the big man as he paused and checked the rugged chronometer on his wrist.

"You've still got four minutes to make your decision. I promised you that much," he said curtly.

"I'm not the enemy. This is more than just about a story. Do you think you can do everything by yourself?" she challenged.

Bolan remained as silent as his namesake as he pulled off his battle harness. He slipped on a pair of jeans over the skin-tight leggings of his blacksuit, then slid the Jericho into its holster and cinched the belt tightly. He unhooked his shoulder holster from its place on the combat harness and slipped it and the sleek machine pistol that it housed across his broad back. A rumpled leather jacket came out of his war bag, and he threw it on over the outfit. "Three minutes."

He busied himself, snapping on a sheath for a concealed knife and spare magazines for his two handguns as well.

"Can I at least lead you to the warehouse? I'll hang back," Abood said. "I promise not to get in the middle of a firefight."

Bolan remained tight-lipped for a few moments. He snapped the folding stock shut on his AK and slipped it into the bag. He glanced at her.

"Give me your rifle," Bolan said.

"How am I going to protect myself?" Abood demanded, gripping the AK more tightly.

"You have your pistol," he answered. "Besides, if you're going to walk through the streets of Van with me, I'd rather you not attract a lot of attention carrying a loaded rifle."

Abood looked down at the ugly weapon in her hands, then surrendered it to him. "So I can take you there?"

"Don't get in my way," he said, finger aimed at her. "And keep your head down."

Abood nodded. "You're in charge."

Bolan folded his arms across his muscular chest. Under the jacket, the blacksuit looked like a skintight T-shirt, the kind that weight lifters wore to show off their well-honed torsos. His words helped to distract her from the way he seemed poured into his jeans.

"You're right. I'm in charge. And no mention of my involvement in the story," Bolan explained. "I have people who can squelch the story if anything comes out. I'd hate to see you waste your time."

Abood held up her hands in surrender. "I don't even have a camera. Your secrets are safe with me. I'll take them to the grave."

Bolan's jaw tightened.

"Sorry, poor choice of words," Abood apologized.

"This isn't a joke," Bolan stated. "This is real."

"Yeah. I have the bruises to prove it," Abood agreed. "You're forgetting that I'm not a tenderfoot."

Bolan's ice-blue eyes narrowed. He wasn't amused.

"You'll be kept confidential," Abood stated. "Anything you let slip—"

"I won't."

Abood swallowed. He'd been so friendly nearly an hour before, prior to her wanting to deal herself into the recovery of the missing medical supplies. But, from what he'd said, she understood the change in tone. He'd been expecting to drop her off, safe and sound with no worries. Now, he was going to bring her close to the flames, and he didn't want her wings to ignite if she got too close. He'd taken responsibility for her, just like he'd taken on the sole responsibility of recovering the drugs.

Abood had heard rumors across the years of such lone wolves, solitary crusaders reporters had occasionally run across. He was like a guardian angel, drawn to the most dangerous spots on Earth, performing good deeds, saving lives and providing aggressive, decisive strikes to those who would harm others.

Abood understood. There was something about the man called Colonel Stone that inspired her to feel not only loyalty, but the desire to protect him. She thought maybe it was because she was a reporter who hunted out the truth and fought for justice in her own way. He was on the same side, waging the same struggle as she did, except with force of will and arms instead of words. Either way, they were both working toward the same cause.

"Thanks for letting me help out, Stone," Abood said softly.

"Call me Brandon," Bolan said. "Sorry for being such an ass, but it's for your own good."

"I know," Abood replied.

"All right. Can you hold the bag?" he asked her. "It's heavy, but…"

"I'll manage," Abood said. She took it, and sure enough it was about as heavy as her dad's range bag when he went to test rifles and pistols for his gun rags. It was nothing she wasn't used to. "What are you going to do?"

Bolan winked. "I'm going to borrow some wheels."

"Yeah, I got the bag. See if you can get something nice, like a Corvette," Abood quipped.

"I'll see what I can do—"

The ground vibrated beneath her feet, and she looked down. Bolan whipped around and looked at the city as the tremors grew in force.

"Earthquake!" he growled.

Suddenly the dirt at her feet heaved, and a fissure opened up between her feet. She lunged forward, and Stone caught her as soil cascaded into the crack in the earth. The pair lurched away as fast as they could on the flexing ground, and at one point, the dirt seemed to disappear beneath their bicycling feet, only to surge up again and knock Abood to her knees. Bolan tumbled forward, heaved off balance by the surging hillside.

A slope suddenly deepened as the earth continued to flex, and Abood let go of the bag to reach for Stone.

The big man skidded down the slippery slope toward a crack in the ground that yawned and snapped shut, like a pair of gigantic jaws.

5

Jandarma Major Omar Baydur arrived in his jeep, looking at the aftermath of the battle between his men and the Kurds.

"Major," one of his men said. He managed to stand at attention, though his right arm hung limply, soaked with blood.

"What happened here?" Baydur asked.

"We lost track of the American journalist. She was taken by a stranger," the wounded officer stated. "Captain Makal gave us the description over the radio."

"Where is Makal?" Baydur asked.

"He continued pursuit overland. It appears that Abood and the stranger took off toward Van."

Baydur frowned. "And what was his progress on the Kongra-Gel search?"

Another Jandarma trooper raised his hand. Baydur recognized this one as Gogin, Makal's most trusted lieutenant. A white bandage covered a bloody thigh wound.

"We had interrogated a suspect, but the journalist interfered before we could get any results," Gogin stated. "We think that the man who snatched that witch Abood might be working with the PKK."

"So why did the Kongras attack him?" the soldier with the injured arm asked.

"The Kongras shot at the man who had the journalist?" Baydur asked.

"Nobody saw for certain," Gogin growled. "Besides, that bastard killed Etter and the others."

"We heard. Four men killed, and Makal retreated to find you," Baydur stated. "You took that bullet in the leg when the Kongras attacked?"

Gogin nodded.

"Strange," Baydur said with a frown. "You seem to be walking pretty well."

"It went clean through," Gogin explained.

"I don't see a bloodstain for the exit wound," Baydur stated. "And if it bled that much in this short a time—"

The earth rumbled, cutting off the Jandarma commander. Trees shook and birds took to the air en masse. It felt like a bomb had gone off nearby, but Baydur had lived through enough earthquakes to realize what was happening. He struggled to stay upright, and Gogin collapsed against the fender of the jeep, wincing in pain.

The radio went wild with cries of alarm. The tremors rose in intensity, and Baydur held on to his vehicle's frame. After what seemed an eternity, the earthquake abated.

"What happened?" Gogin asked, sliding to a half-seated position on the hood of the jeep.

"An earthquake. It was either a small, local one—" Baydur began.

"Sir!" Sezer, his driver, interrupted. "The radio waves are crowded, but the closest I can make out is that Van was hit again. Something big."

Baydur got into the jeep. "A bomb?"

"Earthquake. As much as I can tell from all the chatter, the landlines have been knocked out," Sezer answered.

"All right, try to get through on our secure lines. We're pulling everyone we have to pitch in with the city," Baydur said.

"What about the bastard who killed our men?" Gogin asked.

"Get off my hood," Baydur answered. "This whole mess has the stink of someone wanting to get back at Makal for one of his antics. I swear—"

Gogin glared. "Swear what? This animal murdered our own people."

"I swear, if I find out that Makal's stepped out of line, and you're helping to cover for it, you're going down a very deep hole," Baydur threatened.

"Sure. Coddle the Commies," Gogin snarled as he slipped off the jeep's hood. "Makal gets results."

Baydur stared back coldly. Sezer threw the jeep into reverse, and the two Turks maintained their glaring contest until the driver spun the vehicle around and turned toward Van.

Kandilli Observatory and Earthquake Research Institute

VIGO PEPIS COULD ONLY watch in impotent horror as the seismic graph for the Lake Van region suddenly shook off the charts. He shot a glance at Bursa, who swallowed hard.

"It's at 7.4 and rising," Zapel spoke up as she read off the graph paper. The needle was going wild. "Seven-five—"

"Oh my God," Bursa gasped in helplessness. "The minister of the interior just told me that they've lost landline communications with Van."

Pepis could only stare as the needle hit 7.7, and the line still didn't stop increasing in the violence of its activity. Radio transponders on seismic sensors enabled them to keep up with current data, simply because of the vulnerability of landlines to tremors.

He thought about the region. Van was one of the primary capitals in Turkish Kurdistan, a city of more than two hundred thousand souls, and in one of the most hotly contested parts of the country. Conflicts between the Jandarma and the Kurdish separatists were furious, resulting in thousands of refugees.

It was the bombing of the relief workers that had masked the initial tremors leading up to this earthquake, leaving Pepis alone and unconfirmed as a prophet of doom. Now, the horrors were coming true, and he couldn't tear his eyes away from the needle. It was a defense mechanism, because if he took his eyes off the harshly scribbled ink on the graph paper, he'd think of the ancient city, its people and all that it had suffered before.

Van had seen endless tragedy over the centuries, from when it was first founded, eight hundred years before the birth of Christ. The most blatant horror was the deportation of millions of Armenians from the region, resulting in the deaths of more than half a million refugees, through violence or starvation. Since then, it had only been more of the same, in smaller quantities, but with no less anger or hatred. Now, nearly a quarter of a million people had been struck by the fist of an angry God. Though they were on one of Asia's largest lakes, Lake Van's brackish waters were useless for either drinking or irrigation.

"The minister of the interior is on line three," Zapel announced.

Bursa picked up the phone and spoke in hushed, hurried tones, then hung up.

"Vigo, the military is unable to assist," he confided. "Whatever is on hand is all that they have."

"If the desalinization plants weren't affected, there might be hope," Pepis stated. "Otherwise—"

"The minister wants to know how bad the aftershocks will be," Bursa cut him off.

"It'll be bad. At least in the six range," Pepis said.

"It went all the way up to 7.83," Zapel announced. "But it's starting to die down."

"It's going to be hell there," Bursa said numbly.

Pepis turned away from the graph.

6

Mack Bolan's left hand dug into the loose soil, but his right hand dropped instinctively to the Ka-Bar fighting knife he'd bought earlier that morning. The blade sank into the earth and dragged for a few moments, but finally his slide toward the chomping rift below him slowed. He dug the toes of his boots into the ground and he hauled with all of his might. His war bag skidded closer to the edge, and for a moment he reached out for it before the earth seized shut, smashing the bag between stony jaws.

The earth stopped heaving, and Bolan drew back, looking at the satchel clamped in the fissure. He winced as a flood of granite pebbles and dust hit him, eyes snapping shut to protect the vulnerable orbs beneath his lids.

"Brandon!" Abood called. He looked up to see the young woman extending one long leg toward him. "Grab my leg!"

Bolan hauled himself up on the knife and grabbed her ankle. With the extra leverage, he managed to crawl to the lip of the cliff. Abood slid back from the edge and sighed.

"We lost the rifles," Bolan announced.

"Are you all right?" she asked.

"No permanent damage," he answered as he looked toward the fissure. He could see a half-loaded box of ammunition sprawled in the dirt, bullets glinting in the sun.

"How much do you have?" Abood asked.

Bolan checked his harness. "Four loaded magazines for the Jericho, and four more for my own Beretta."

"You usually carry all that ammo?" Abood asked. She shook her head. "Sorry…I forgot. You're a spook in hostile territory."

"I'll get by," Bolan said. He looked around, then grabbed the root of a tree trunk, stretched down and pulled his knife out of the dirt. "It's not worth the risk to climb down to grab more ammo, but the knife will be useful."

Bolan looked toward the city. In the frantic slide to death when the ground first shook, he'd only been concerned about keeping himself and Abood alive. Now, the city of Van had changed drastically from when he'd seen it only moments before. Columns of thick, choking smoke rose lazily into the sky from fires. Clouds of gray-white dust from collapsed buildings formed a hazy fog in the wake of the brutal earthquake.

"Good God," Abood whispered.

Bolan couldn't speak. Already his mind was racing. He was going to have to navigate through a city where buildings had been compromised. He knew that in the aftermath of such violent earthquakes, lethal aftershocks ripped through the terrain, causing nearly as much damage when shifting earth gave that one final tug that brought down weakened buildings and power lines, or split streets to expose jets of invisible, highly flammable gas into the air. In all of the Executioner's years of warfare, he had seen only a few cities as thoroughly destroyed, and usually those were the targets of coordinated, concentrated bombing, and the destruction was spread over hours, not moments.

"We've got to do something," Abood said, breaking the numbed silence.

"We don't have anything to help them with," Bolan answered. "Unless we recover those medical supplies."

"Don't you have contact with your superiors?" Abood asked.

"No. I was en route from another mission," Bolan said. "This was sort of a pickup."

Abood looked at him in disbelief.

"If the law finds out that I'm intruding in their territory, there will be hell to pay," Bolan admitted. "Which was why—"

"Which was why you didn't want me along," Abood concluded. "One of the reasons, at least. Your mystery bosses give you carte blanche in racking up collateral damage?"

"No, my boss doesn't want any collateral damage at all," Bolan answered firmly.

Abood narrowed her eyes. "Something tells me that I'm looking at your only boss right now."

"Are you going to conduct an interview, or do we find those stolen medical supplies and save a few thousand people?" Bolan asked.

Abood grimaced for a moment, then her irritation dissolved and she smiled softly. "You got me there, soldier."

"Come on," Bolan said. "It's fifteen minutes by brisk walk to the closest street. If we run, we can find some wheels and get those medical supplies even more quickly."

The Executioner turned toward a safe path down the cliff and started jogging.

Abood was right on his heels.

Stony Man Farm, Virginia

"A FEW MINUTES BEFORE the earthquake, we picked this up," Barbara Price said as she handed the translation to Hal Brognola.

"Tall man, six, to six-and-a-half-feet tall, heavily armed, indeterminate nationality," Brognola murmured as he read it. "Who put out the word?"

"That was under Jandarma's known frequencies," Price answered. "Bear thought it best to keep our ears open on the police scanners, give Striker a bit of assistance in the region if he should call in."

Brognola frowned. "I wished he'd taken the time to hook up properly with us before tearing off after the Kongras."

Price sighed and folded her arms. "Striker said that time was of the essence. The Kongras wouldn't hold on to the stolen medical supplies for more than forty-eight hours, maybe even less. He said he had to be on the ground and operating before they had a chance to move that stuff out to the black market."

Brognola squeezed the wrinkled knot between his eyebrows, then blinked away his frustration.

"Hal, you've known him longer than almost anyone," Price said. "You know that Mack isn't going to turn his back when he can do some good. Now, it's even more vital than ever for him to get those relief supplies."

"How bad was the earthquake?" Brognola asked.

"Kandilli Research Institute measured it at 7.8," Price responded. She set aerial photographs of the city of Van in front of Brognola.

"Christ, it looks like it's been hit by a bomb," the big Fed stated.

"According to Aaron, a 7.8 earthquake is nearly as powerful as the bomb that hit Hiroshima," Price stated. "Or it at least released the same amount of energy as an atomic weapon."

Brognola shook his head. "What do we have in the region that can help out?"

"Not much. Turkey is still sensitive about the Iraq invasion, so our resources in the area have been drastically trimmed," Price stated. "Politics will keep people dragging their feet, and even if there was a way to get major supplies in, it would still take at least three days before we could have a strong enough presence there."

"What would we be talking about?" Brognola asked.

"The President has two aircraft carriers he can deploy," Price stated. "One off Kuwait, and one in the Mediterranean. Between their desalinization plants, they can airlift enough fresh water to turn the tide."

"Airlift fresh water?" Brognola asked. "There's a huge lake right near the city."

"It's a saltwater lake," Price answered. "It's not fit for drinking or irrigation. The best we can hope for is for one carrier to make port in Iskenderun and ferry supplies across four hundred miles of Turkish airspace."

Brognola pursed his lips. "And the Turkish government is still sensitive about our craft using their airspace to penetrate Iraq airspace. "All right. What about the teams? Can we dispatch them to give Striker some backup?"

"Able Team and Phoenix Force are fully occupied. Able Team would be free in thirty-six hours, then factoring in travel time…. There's nothing we can send right away," Price stated.

"None of our assets in the region are available?" Brognola asked. "We have former blacksuits in every branch of the military and a lot of embassy posts."

"Nobody on hand," Price admitted. "Our military people have their work cut out for them, and any who would be dispatched to the scene are going to be busy with conventional relief efforts."

Brognola picked up his cigar and began chewing on it to relieve his frustration. It took a moment for the old stress mechanisms to take effect, and his mind cleared. "Just keep your ears open for Striker. You never know. He might be able to contact us. I want the cyberteam to give him every assistance and up-to-date satellite intel. Paths through the city, aftershock warnings, what we hear from the Jandarma…"

Price nodded.

Brognola looked at the translation. "He killed them while they were questioning an American journalist."

"You know how the Turkish paramilitary forces work, Hal. If Striker dropped the hammer on them, the only questions asked were 'who do you want to rape you first' or 'head or gut, where do you want to be shot?'"

"Yeah. It's just going to make things a lot more difficult if we have to call in some favors to help him out," Brognola stated.

"I put the word out to our people. If anyone's cozy with the Jandarma, we won't ask them for help. It'll narrow down our resources, but…"

"Just do it," Brognola said. "I'll inform the President that we have Striker on the ground."

"Hal," Barbara spoke up.

"Mack will be okay. He's been hunted by far worse than the Kongras and the Jandarma."

"The Mafia and the KGB might have had better technology, but the Kongras and the Jandarma are as brutal as anything he's ever faced," Price stated. "They'll peel a man alive for a week just to make him hurt."

Brognola looked back at the photos. "You don't make reassuring you any easier."

Price nodded. "Reassurance is one thing. Outright lying is another."

Brognola frowned. "If Striker's alive, he'll make it through. It's what he does. He's survived on his own for so long…."

The head Fed's words trailed off as he looked at the stricken city in the photograph. If Mack Bolan had survived the earthquake, he'd do as much as he could to recover the relief supplies and save the shattered people of Van. Bolan was a man who would move heaven and earth to save lives, no matter what odds were stacked against him.

But Brognola realized full well that with two renegade paramilitary armies, and the aftermath of an earthquake against him, the Executioner was in for the struggle of his life.

7

The first car they found was unlocked, and Mack Bolan counted himself lucky. He knew the faster he could cut across Van, the more lives he could save. He threw open the door and even though no keys were in the ignition, he had hot-wired enough automobiles to do it on autopilot. He stabbed his knife into the steering column and tore away its plastic housing when he heard a faint distant cry.

"What's wrong?" Abood asked.

"I heard something," Bolan answered. He put his fingers to his lips and concentrated. He heard the call for help again and got out of the car.

"Someone is going to ask us what we're doing around this car," Abood stated.

Abood was right. The longer it took to steal the automobile, the more chance they would be caught by Jandarma forces on patrol. But if there was someone in danger, Bolan's instincts called for him to do something.

"Stay with the car," Bolan said. He stripped the wires and sparked them together. The car turned over in an instant. "Drive it around the block. I'm going to look for the source of those cries."

Bolan turned from the car as Abood scooted into the driver's seat and gunned the engine. "Stone—"

"I'll be careful," Bolan told her. "Just keep the car warm."

Abood nodded and Bolan strode off, loping along at a ground-eating pace. He immediately saw where the cries originated from. A small girl stood alone, in the doorway of a half-collapsed apartment building. She turned and saw Bolan jogging toward her and her eyes widened, afraid.

Bolan slowed and held his hands out carefully and gently, speaking low and soft, in English, but hoping that his tone would translate until he figured out what language the girl spoke. "No, it's okay. I'm here to help."

The girl took a tentative step back, then pointed inside. She said something, only two syllables, but it was enough. "Ma-ma."

Bolan nodded and followed the girl as she led him through a hallway. It was choked with rubble, and there seemed to be no way past. Through the barrier, however, he could hear the plaintive screams of a woman calling for help, deadened by the weight of collapsed stone. The girl spoke up, rattling off in rapid Turkish.

The woman didn't stop screaming, and Bolan wondered if she could hear clearly. He gestured to the girl to cover her ears. She did and then in his best parade march bellow, he called out. "Can you hear me?"

The woman stopped. Garbled Turkish erupted. Bolan knew a few words in the language, but the gist was lost on him. She repeated one word several times—"Lata."

Bolan knew the Turkish word for "help"; it was one of the phrases he memorized before cutting across the border. "Lata" sounded like a name.

He looked down at the girl. "Lata?"

The girl nodded.

Bolan searched his memory for a moment and then pulled up the Turkish phrase he needed. He barked it out loudly, Lata covering her ears again. "Lata's safe!"

The woman on the other side broke down in a mixture of

tears and laughter, the sounds of relief cutting through the heavy rubble. Bolan tested the barrier and pulled his flashlight. Its bright beam cut into the darkness above, and he knew that several levels had collapsed onto this hallway. The heavy floors made it impossible to move, as they had wedged down tightly. He'd need another way to get to the trapped woman.

Bolan turned, his mind racing. Picking an apartment door, he kicked it open violently. Wood splintered and the door swung open. No one was inside. The ceiling had buckled in a few places, and in the direction of the woman, he noticed that the wall had crumbled at the top. He pulled the all-steel Jericho pistol and hammered it against the cracked drywall. The girl gasped in surprise that he was armed, but saw what he was doing and calmed down. After three hard taps, there was a fist-sized hole in the drywall, and he could see through to the next apartment.

Bolan took a firm grasp of the drywall and cracked a chunk free easily. He holstered the Jericho and tapped the wall, checking for the width of the support studs, then hurled himself against it with all his might. Drywall crumbled under his weight, and he dented the far side.

"Thanks for cheap apartment construction," he muttered. The girl took a tentative step forward and Bolan rammed the half-broken wall again and burst through. Covered in plaster and powdered drywall, he looked around the next apartment. His shoulder ached from where he'd used it as an improvised wrecking ball. He looked back at Lata, who watched him in awe.

The apartment's ceiling was buckled in several places, and a sofa from an upstairs apartment poked through into the room. It wouldn't be safe for the little girl. Bolan knelt and motioned for her to stay put in the doorway they'd come through. If the floor was going to collapse, that would be a safer place for her. Lata nodded in understanding and ran to where he pointed.

"Thank you," she said in Turkish. Bolan understood and smiled, then tried the apartment door.

It opened a couple of inches but was stopped by a massive weight on the other side. Bolan braced the door with one hand, then drew his Jericho again, and its solid steel frame cracked the wood with one hammer blow. Bolan holstered the weapon, then used his forearm to drive the broken section of door away. He could see into the hallway, and the woman lying on the floor. She was wedged under a support pillar. He could see that her scalp was split, and that blood soaked down into one of her ears. No wonder she hadn't heard the little girl's voice. It had taken Bolan's volume to cut through her partial deafness.

Her eyes were glazed, and she was starting to slip into shock. Bolan grabbed the door frame and pulled hard. After his third tug, the molding around the door ripped free and clattered to the floor at his feet. Plaster rained from the ceiling above, and the Executioner knew that he wouldn't have much time. He considered using a gun to shoot out the hinges, but the percussion would weaken the ceiling more. Instead, he took out his knife and pried the top hinge. Cheap brass folded under its leverage. Held in place by only one hinge, and unrestrained by the door frame's molding, he'd be able to wrench the bottom hinge loose. With a powerful tug, his shoulders and back protesting against the effort, he tore the half-broken door free, using the space he'd smashed out of its corner as a handle.

Bolan scanned the area, then grabbed a chair and wedged the door into it and up against the ceiling. It wouldn't last for long, but he hoped it would buy him a few minutes. He knelt by the woman's side. He took her dark, bloodied hand in his and gave it a gentle squeeze.

"I'm here to help," he said as he looked at the weight holding her in place.

"Lata?" the woman inquired. Her voice cracked, barely above a whisper. She'd worn out her vocal cords crying for her child. Bolan dug his fingers in under the support pillar and tried to lift it, but he couldn't move it. If he could get a quarter inch of slack, the woman would have been able to crawl out to safety. But there just was too much rubble wedging it down.

The mother looked through the door, her eyes widening fearfully. "Lata!"

Bolan looked back and saw the little girl.

The woman clutched at his leg. She shook her head.

Bolan took a deep breath, grimacing at the woman's implications. She wanted him to take Lata and escape before the whole building came down. Plaster rained on the little girl and she screamed. Bolan rose to his feet and scooped Lata out of the way as the sofa crashed to the floor from the apartment above.

In his rush to rescue the little girl, he didn't feel the tremors of the aftershock immediately. The woman winced as the weight pressed against her. Bolan pushed Lata into the gap he'd made to the next apartment.

"Stay," he told her firmly in simple Turkish. He looked around. He couldn't give up on this girl's mother. Then he saw the kitchenette by the door. He strode over and opened the cabinets and found several bottles. He couldn't tell what they were exactly, their labels unintelligible, but one he saw had bubbles, and another was a form of greasy oil. He pocketed five bottles of various soaps and oils, then looked around. He could make it more slippery for the mother to slide out, but he needed leverage. The pillar that wedged her in had shifted, which meant it could now be moved, but its weight could crush her if he slipped. He saw a coatrack and tested it. It was a chunk of solid wood, and Bolan kicked off the flimsy hooks on one end before slipping through the doorway.

The injured woman looked at him, frightened. Bolan gave her a nod, then drove the shaft of the coatrack under the pillar. Bracing the wood across his hip, he plucked out the bottles and pulled off their tops. Greasy, slippery fluids poured onto the floor, soaking beneath the trapped woman. She squirmed, but when her shoulders slipped loosely, without any traction, understanding crossed her features.

Bolan pushed all his weight into lifting the wedged pillar. The coatrack's shaft started to crackle under the strain. The woman gasped as the weight stopped pressing on her.

"Now!" Bolan ordered, keeping his muscle pressed into his improvised lever. She fumbled and slipped, then pushed against the thing that had trapped her, and found the leverage to slide free. Lata rushed to the doorway and took her mother's hand, and the Turkish mother and daughter stumbled back into the apartment as the wood snapped against Bolan's shoulder.

The Executioner staggered back, and the pillar hammered into the floor. A wash of rubble assaulted his legs, but he managed to kick free.

Lata was leading her mother to the next apartment when Bolan caught up with them and steered them toward the window. With a powerful kick, he shattered the glass and, using the fallen sofa's cushion, swept away broken shards to make it safe for them. They slipped out and Bolan dived through just as the ceiling came down on the heels of another aftershock.

The woman wrapped her arms around Bolan's neck and kissed his cheek, tears flowing.

Abood pulled up in their stolen car, and Bolan knew that he couldn't leave these two behind.

"We've got passengers," he told Abood. He gestured for the Turkish refugees to climb into the back seat.

"I thought you were in a hurry," Abood said, looking back at Lata, who rewarded the journalist with a bright smile.

Bolan refused to take the bait and slid into the shotgun seat. "We'll drop them off and recover the medical supplies."

Abood nodded.

The stolen car raced through the streets.

8

Captain Yuli Makal heard his cell phone warble and he plucked it from his pocket. He recognized the number. It was Gogin. "What's wrong?"

"Baydur. He's joined the chase for our mystery shooter."

"Damn—"

"He didn't buy the story about me getting hit during the mix-up with the Kongras," Gogin explained. "That politically correct bastard is going to know something's up when he finds out that Abood was armed. He might match up that it was her pistol bullet, not a Kongra-rifle slug, in my leg."

"You got rid of the round, though, didn't you?" Makal asked. Out the window, the Turkish countryside raced past. In the distance, smoke rose from the wreckage of Van, and his stomach knotted.

"Yes. It hurt badly when Sengor pulled it out, but Baydur isn't going to find her 9 mm," Gogin said. "We're clean on that for now. But he's going to try to take Abood and the mystery man alive."

"He killed four Jandarma, and she shot you. They're not going to take the Americans alive," Makal answered. "If the West wants to give those Communist pieces of trash a soapbox to stand on, let them. That soapbox is going to be their coffin."

"You're going to leave that much for them?" Gogin asked with a chuckle.

"Maybe less," Makal answered. "Keep me up-to-date on how Baydur's doing. You can hobble around, right?"

"Yeah, but then the earthquake hit. Baydur made it a priority for the Jandarma to assist in search and rescue efforts. Finding our people is on the back burner for them," Gogin stated.

"So that gives me some breathing room," Makal concluded. "Good. Keep your nose clean, and don't give Baydur any reason to think that he's— Gogin?"

Makal looked down and realized that his cell phone had lost its signal. He sighed. Service only recently installed around the city had been spotty in the first place. The earthquake had to have left entire areas blacked out, and Makal would be cut off from his lieutenant. He turned to the rest of his crew in the vehicle.

"All right," Makal told them. "We're not going to be able to talk to Gogin reliably. Some cell-phone towers have been taken out by the earthquake. We're not completely on our own, but we'd better watch our step. That coward Baydur doesn't have the nerve to do what has to be done to stop the Commies. So, we have to find Abood and get the location of the warehouse out of her before she or the Kongras get to it."

"What if the bitch won't talk?" Sengor asked.

Makal flicked open his knife, then closed it. "Don't worry. I'll cut right to the heart of the matter."

ABOOD SKIDDED THE CAR to a halt. She'd thrown her photographer's vest over the steering column, and untucked her safari shirt to let it drape over her hips to camouflage that the car was hot-wired. She looked slovenly, but fashion wasn't on her mind. Bolan had doffed his jacket as well, replacing it with a loose shirt that he'd grabbed off a laundry line. That concealed his two handguns and battle harness as well as the leather coat that now kept Lata and her mother, Terenia, warm.

"What's going on here?" the sentry asked as Abood rolled down the window. Since Abood knew the language better than Bolan, she decided to do all the talking.

"My photographer and I ran into these people in a collapsed apartment building," Abood said. "We were bringing them to medical assistance."

The guard looked back to the relief station, then sighed. "We're pretty crowded."

"Don't worry. Brandon managed to clean her wounds and bandage them," Abood explained.

The guard leaned in, and Bolan gave him a friendly smile and a wave.

"Can I see your identification?" the soldier asked.

Abood handed over hers.

"His too," the soldier added.

"He lost it…and his bag in the earthquake," Abood said. "I barely pulled him to safety before the whole place fell down on us. All he has is the shirt on his back."

Bolan turned out his pockets, which were empty, then shrugged.

"Doesn't he speak Turkish?" the soldier asked.

"Do you speak Arabic?" Bolan asked haltingly, in that language.

The soldier frowned. "Yes. What happened?"

"I lost everything trying to help these people. I set down my camera bag to help the woman and her child, and the ceiling collapsed before I could get it back. If Catherine hadn't yanked me through the window—" Bolan shuddered convincingly.

The soldier looked at the people in the back seat. He switched back to Turkish.

"Is what these people are saying true?" the soldier asked.

"Yes!" Lata spoke up. "He saved us! He knocked down a wall and everything!"

Aftershock

Lata flexed her slender arms, as if to show off her muscles.

Abood chuckled.

"So, Mr....?" the soldier asked, returning to Arabic.

"Brandon Stone," Bolan replied. "Just helping out when I can."

"Well, thanks," the soldier answered. "Do you think you can find your hotel? It might still be standing, and it's better than adding four people to this camp."

"All right, sir," Abood said, slipping easily into Arabic as well.

Lata and Terenia got out of the car, and the woman and girl leaned through the window and gave Bolan a grateful hug and a kiss. Bolan and Abood waved goodbye to them.

"I'm sorry," the soldier explained. "We're pretty packed here as it is. You'll probably fend better with the other westerners."

Abood nodded. "I understand."

"Mr. Stone?" the soldier asked.

"Yes, sir?" Bolan waited for the soldier to speak.

"Thanks," the Turk replied.

Bolan extended his hand and the two men shook.

"Good luck," the soldier replied.

Abood pulled away and headed toward her hotel.

"Brandon, we're running low on gas," Abood said. She frowned. "I don't think too many gas stations will be safe."

"No. The underground tanks might have ruptured and leaked," Bolan added. "Look," he said.

A column of fire blazed at the corner of an intersection. Jets of flames spit up from where the gas pumps would have been. Here and there on rooftops, tar paper smoldered where licks and sparks landed from the pillars of fire. People gave the station a wide berth.

"This is some kind of nightmare," Abood said.

The car sputtered and died.

Bolan looked at the dashboard and sighed. "I shouldn't have left you driving around."

"You were saving lives. Don't apologize."

Bolan looked around, trying to figure out where they could get more fuel. The gas station was indicative of the kind of horrors they'd run into if they went to other stations. While they wouldn't necessarily be spewing flames, there would be the danger of sparks, or broken pumps from the earthquake, making it impossible to get more fuel. He scanned the surrounding area. He could siphon fuel from parked vehicles. Finding a length of hose would prove no problem.

The crack of a shotgun down the road cut through his planning instantly.

"Kill the engine and stay put," the Executioner ordered.

More gunfire barked, fast and furious. Not quite full-auto, but enough to tell Bolan that there was more than one gunman.

"More trouble," Abood murmured. "Let me—"

"Stay put and guard the car," Bolan said sharply as he slid out the passenger door, USP Compact in hand. "This might be a distraction. Besides, if I'm lucky, I might get us something more substantial than our pistols."

Abood nodded and disconnected the ignition wires. The engine died and she eased her hand under her open blouse, fingers wrapping around the thin rubber grips of her customized Beretta.

Bolan raced along, pistol aimed at the ground, finger resting along the frame over the trigger guard. The 9 mm gun had no safety catch, but it would only fire with a deliberate pull of the trigger. He didn't want a stumble to discharge his pistol unintentionally. He tucked himself in a doorway and saw a trio of ragged-looking gunmen, armed with pistols and a shotgun, exchanging fire with someone hidden in a storefront.

Looters.

Bolan brought the pistol to bear, then lowered it. The gun was accurate, but the range was nearly forty yards to the concealed gunmen. The pistol fired 9 mm hardball ammo, which would limit the gun's stopping power. He holstered the weapon and pulled out the more powerful Jericho. It would give him better reach, and the heavy barrel and frame made the .40-caliber handgun as accurate as it could be. He snicked off the safety, rested the silhouette of his front sight on the lower back of the shotgunner and eased back the hammer.

The shotgunner pumped his weapon again and took aim, and Bolan took that moment to trigger the Jericho. It roared once, a heavy-caliber slug crashing into the looter's spine and shattering it on impact. The other two gunmen whirled as their friend fell, and Bolan swept the Jericho to chest level. He tapped out two more shots that punched into the chest of a predator who had spotted him before his partner. Both flat-point rounds hammered into the Turkish outlaw's rib cage and threw him onto his back.

Bullets bounced off the ground as the second gunner triggered his weapon too low. One of the slugs knifed across Bolan's thigh before the Executioner triggered a round into the looter's throat. The jacketed lead shoveled through the would-be killer's windpipe and burst in a gory mess through his neck bones.

Bolan was about to take a step forward when a man stood in the window of the store. The store owner worked desperately with the bolt action of his rifle, then saw Bolan step into the open, pistol pointed skyward, other hand empty.

"Go away!" the Turk shouted. He levered the jammed rifle at Bolan's chest, but he didn't have a good grip on the weapon. "Go away!"

Bolan stopped his approach, and realized that the man was too frightened to comprehend the Executioner was there to help. He put the Jericho away in its holster, then turned and walked back to the car. He didn't look back as he finally heard the panicked store owner chamber a round into his rifle.

Bolan realized that even a half-empty shotgun would have given them an edge in case they'd run across Jandarma shock troopers on the hunt, but he wasn't going to antagonize a frightened defender by looting for firepower.

Abood looked at him from behind the steering wheel as she twisted the ignition wires together.

"What happened?" she asked.

"Someone thought they could get a 9 mm discount at a store," Bolan said, getting into the car. He sat back.

"You didn't get anything?" Abood continued.

"It wasn't worth the risk to press the issue," Bolan explained. "We'll have to keep our eyes open. We not only have Kongras and Jandarma, but there are looters as well. And stealing a car might be dangerous."

"The citizens are over their shock, and those sticking by their homes aren't going to take too kindly to thieves," Abood said.

"Exactly," Bolan answered.

Abood stepped on the gas pedal, but the car sputtered and died. She tried the ignition wires again, but there wasn't even a spark as they touched. "Great. Battery died."

"We wouldn't have been able to get much farther," Bolan conceded. "Let's go."

Abood got out of the car, tucked in her blouse, then put on her photographer's vest. She looked back toward where Bolan had his firefight. "Can't go that way."

Bolan looked at the blazing gas station. "We'll cut back and cross over a couple blocks."

He looked at her. "Down that road is a direct line to the warehouse, isn't it?"

Abood nodded. "Yeah."

Bolan looked back in that direction. "So who did you find that out from?"

"I have my confidential sources," Abood said, walking. Bolan had no trouble keeping up with her pace, even though she walked angrily at a ground-eating rate.

Bolan took a deep breath. "It was a relative of the teenaged boy the Jandarma tortured and murdered," he said.

"Good guess," Abood answered.

"But the boy had nothing to do with the theft. He just happened to have the wrong last name. So you're angry at those thugs," Bolan added.

"I'm sure you have no qualms about torturing information out of someone," Abood growled.

"There's a difference between questioning someone who might know something and putting the screws to someone who was directly involved," Bolan replied. "The Jandarma crossed a line I never would."

"That's easy to say—"

"I've been around long enough to know that torture might work, but it takes too long and is far too unreliable," Bolan said.

"They didn't have to do that to him," Abood snarled, trying to use her anger to disguise a sob. "I shot one of those scumbags in the leg and took off before they could spot me."

"That doesn't sound like impartial and balanced journalism," Bolan quipped.

"No. And while it was stupid, it was my fault they did that to Recep," Abood stated.

"The boy they tortured."

"They handcuffed him to a pipe, and Makal was cutting strips out of his chest with a knife," Abood said. She stopped walking, and she started to close her eyes, but stopped.

Bolan knew it was because every time she shut them, she

could see the image of the young man being brutalized by Jandarma thugs. The emotional wounds were too fresh in Abood's mind to sublimate them. It had been only hours since the atrocity.

A tear crawled down her cheek, and her lips twisted angrily. "They'd exposed half of his chest. Every time they cut loose skin, they'd burn it with a blast of flame from an aerosol can and lighter, cauterizing him so he wouldn't bleed to death. So he'd live long enough to tell him what they wanted." Abood's right hand had clenched into a fist, her knuckles white with rage.

Bolan remained silent, knowing that she was volatile right now. One wrong word, and he'd never be able to recover the trust he'd gained with her. He needed her knowledge to reach the medical supplies first, before the Jandarma or the Kongras.

Abood looked up, noting Bolan's silence and the look of concern on his face. "I was the one who'd led Makal to Recep." She winced. "Recep had found out where the Kongras had hidden the supplies. He found out from his cousin Boz, who was in on the heist."

She looked away. "Recep told me, and I was on my way to the warehouse. I forgot my notebook, and when I came back, they had him cuffed. I stood for minutes, just watching... I didn't know what to do."

Bolan reached out to rest a comforting hand on her shoulder, but she jerked away.

"I stood still, stupid, not knowing what to do. He was crying, screaming, and I was paralyzed. By the time I got up the nerve, he was mutilated beyond any hope of repair, skinned and burned..."

Abood's hand waved at the space between her and Bolan, as if warding him off. "I shot one of those bastards. I was aiming for his pelvis—"

She looked up. "Not to shoot him in the balls—"

Bolan nodded. "To cripple him. Break his pelvis. Make him into a victim."

"Yeah," Abood answered. "To let him live the rest of his life, weak and mutilated. Just like Recep…if he recovered. I told them to cut him down. I had the drop on those freaks, none of them had their guns out, their rifles were propped in the corner."

"You did what you could," Bolan said.

"Makal cut down Recep," Abood continued. "He cut Recep down with a bullet in the head. And he told me I was next. I shot, but I don't know if I hit anyone. I shot and ran, but they caught up with me."

Bolan gently took Abood's hand, and she tried to twist away. "You tried to help him," he said.

"I got him killed. I got him tortured. It was my fault," Abood answered as Bolan slid his arm around her shoulders. She started shaking.

"You tried to help him," Bolan whispered.

She balled up her fist and struck him in the chest, a hard punch making him wince, a blow thrown from frustration. She hammered him three more times before she slumped against him, breaking down in tears.

"I should…I should have…I know things…I know how to…"

Bolan wrapped both arms around her, pinning and trapping her, more for her protection than his own. He hurt from where she'd battered him, but he was concerned that she might take out her anger on herself. She trembled from a mixture of rage and sorrow.

Abood's tears finally stopped, her sobbing and struggles calmed down, and Bolan loosened his embrace.

"You've been there too," Abood said.

Bolan nodded.

"Does it ever stop hurting?"

Bolan shook his head.

"Then what do you do?"

"You help others so they don't feel like you do," Bolan answered.

"Does that help you forgive yourself?"

Bolan stepped away from Abood. "It's not about forgiving myself. And it shouldn't be about you forgiving yourself. You weren't the killer. You didn't hurt him. You were there to save his life, and you did everything you could. And right now, what you need to do is make certain that his death wasn't in vain."

"The medical supplies," Abood said softly.

Bolan rested a hand on her shoulder. "Others can be saved."

Abood nodded, still numb. Her pain hadn't abated, but her reason had once again asserted itself. "Thanks, Brandon."

"Don't worry about it," Bolan replied. "Come on."

Abood and the Executioner continued walking toward the warehouse.

The doomsday numbers still ticked down.

9

Boz Arcuri looked around his family home, livid with rage. His young cousin lay in the middle of the floor, mutilated and executed by point-blank gunfire. Arcuri's jaw clenched tightly as he knelt by Recep and stroked his dark, blood spattered hair.

"Recep, why did you have to get involved?" he said with a sad shake of his head.

A dark, glassy eye reflected his own features, twisted and disgruntled, and he wondered if in some way that was his answer. He was the one who had berated his uncles for their inactivity against the thuggish murderers that the Turkish government allowed to run wild throughout the countryside. Recep had always shown he'd been a good soul, and always wanted to help.

But Recep's nosiness had caught up with him, and because he knew about the relief-supply theft, he was dead.

"Boz?"

Arcuri spun at the sound of his own name, hand dropping to the pistol in his pocket.

"It's me," Kagan Trug announced. His bodyguards flanked him, and they had Arcuri under their guns. "It's okay, boys."

The bodyguards lowered their weapons, but fingers still rested on triggers. Arcuri released his own gun and stood up.

"I'm sorry about Recep," Trug said, walking forward.

"They tortured the boy. Do you think they found out where we have our supplies hidden?"

"It's possible. Recep told me he wasn't involved, but if the Jandarma butchered him like this, he must have had some kind of information," Arcuri answered. He ground his teeth together.

"We'll get them back," Trug replied. "I recognize this kind of handiwork."

"Me too. Makal, that bastard…"

"His men are trying to clear out our men in order to avoid the new regulations coming down from Ankara," Trug stated. "There's a reformist major in the ranks who doesn't like them to play dirty. But if Makal finds the missing supplies, who knows how he's going to use that information?"

"You think that he might set himself up a nest egg in case they retire him?" Arcuri asked.

"Makal is a gangster with a badge. If they steal that badge, he's going to find his own way to keep his power. What better way than moving in on our big score?"

Arcuri grumbled. "Even if he keeps a handful of the supplies back to sell, claiming we shipped part of it out already, he could convince the government that he's still their golden boy."

"Either way, our only saving grace is that Makal is not enamored of Major Baydur," Trug said.

"Baydur… He'd be almost tolerable if he were to effect his reforms."

"Which is why we're going to make it easier for him," Trug stated, resting his hand on the man's shoulder. "We're going to make sure Makal doesn't get our stash."

Arcuri pursed his lips and looked at Recep's corpse. "So, he lives after he did this to my family?"

Trug sighed. "I don't think that Makal was solely at fault here."

Arcuri's eyes narrowed.

"Recep was talking with an American journalist," Trug announced.

It felt as if a hot slug tore through Arcuri's gut. "What?"

"The reporter, Abood."

Arcuri punched the wall with such violence that the bodyguards raised their weapons again. Trug waved them down. "That bitch. I told her to keep her nose out of Kurdish business."

"What do you expect with a name like Abood?" Trug asked. "She's filthy with Arab blood. Syrian, Iraqi, Saudi, whatever, she's not one of us just because she speaks the language. You know how they hate the Kurdish people."

Arcuri gave the wall a kick as he rubbed his sore fist. "Damn it. Damn that whore—"

"You'll get your chance. She's currently wanted by the Jandarma," Trug said.

Arcuri frowned. "What do you mean?"

"Recep told her everything he knew," Trug stated. "All so she could make a headline over our suffering here."

"Recep is no traitor," Arcuri snapped.

"No, he's not. But these witches have their means. You know full well how they can seduce others into thinking that they are on the side of God and justice. And yet, when they do, what happens?" Trug asked.

"Our people have it no better in Iraq," Arcuri admitted.

"Correct," Trug stated. "They tell pretty lies, but in the end, it's all about their interests and needs."

"So why haven't we captured her?" Arcuri asked.

"Two factors. The earthquake."

"And the other?" Arcuri pressed.

"She hooked up with an intruder," Trug stated. "We believe he might be an American."

"An intruder?"

Trug squeezed a knot in the center of his brow. "This man

attacked our training camp. Dozens died in the conflagration, and he escaped, despite the fact we've caught up with him twice."

Arcuri swallowed. "One man?"

"Yes. Tall. Dark hair and dark skinned, dressed in black and fighting like he was an entire army," Trug continued.

Arcuri's jaw tightened again, and he saw stars as the pressure rose in his skull. "So we have the Jandarma and the Americans against us?"

"There is no indication of any other Americans or other foreigners in the region, at least none who weren't here when we stole the supplies," Trug told him. "We have him outnumbered."

Arcuri nodded. "How many men do we have mobilized?"

"I have a guard force at the warehouse, but many of our people have deserted to help their families," Trug explained.

"That's understandable," Arcuri said. "I came here to check on my family—" Tears stung the man's eyes as he looked down at Recep.

Trug stepped closer to his lieutenant, and wrapped a comforting arm around his shoulders. "Do you want to take some time to bury Recep?"

Arcuri felt a flash of rage pierce him. "Dead is dead. He'll be here tomorrow morning. Abood and the American might flee if we don't capture them."

Trug's mouth tightened into a hard line. "I'll see if I can get someone to take care of him for you."

"Thank you," Arcuri said, pulling away from his commander. "I have work to do."

Arcuri stepped out of the front door and moved toward his pickup truck.

If he looked back, he might have seen a smile split Trug's face.

Instead, Arcuri only saw the blood he was going to spill to avenge his cousin.

"I LET BOZ OFF HIS LEASH," Trug informed Makal over the phone.

"I'm touched that you thought of me first, Kagan," Makal said with a sneer. "You know that Baydur's looking for the first chance at me he can get."

"Arcuri knows that, which is why he's a lot more interested in Abood and her mystery savior," Trug stated. "In Boz's heart, you're already meat on the grill."

Makal cleared his throat. "Yes. It might even be the truth."

"Worried about me, Yuli?"

"When my balls are in someone's pocket, I tend to be a little nervous," Makal explained.

"Mine are in yours as well. If my men knew that I was the one who directed you to torture and kill their loved ones, their friends…"

"Just remember that," Makal answered.

"Just do not grow any idealism on me, partner," Trug stated.

"No. Idealists are cannon fodder for you. You made me into the bogeyman, which was good for my side of the business, but now that reputation has got Ankara hot on my tail, and that idiot Baydur is nipping at me."

"That's the balance of power," Trug stated. "You're too effective for him to go after you immediately. This earthquake is actually a blessing."

Makal looked out the window at the wreckage. "You can call this a blessing?"

"It keeps the investigators on our case occupied," Trug stated.

Makal took a deep breath to hold down his bile. "Your people are out here suffering too."

Trug grunted an affirmative. "What does not kill them only makes them stronger. And your job is secure, so count your blessings."

"And if Arcuri rolls across me?" Makal asked.

"You wipe him out. Boz is skilled, but you are too, and you outnumber him," Trug answered. "But you'll be glad that Arcuri is on the warpath."

"How so?"

Trug paused for a moment on the other end of the line. "Arcuri wants the American."

"He was able to squirm out of both of our forces' grasps."

"Cold feet, Yuli?"

"I'm just concerned about keeping the rest of my carcass warm."

"Arcuri might give you that chance."

"I'll insure my own survival," Makal answered. "You just keep your head, in case the American comes calling for you. Remember, your people killed the relief workers."

"It was Boz who pressed the trigger," Trug said.

"So they'll kill each other?" Makal asked.

"Or leave whoever survives too weak to put up any defense."

Makal sighed.

"Talk to you later, Yuli."

The line went dead, leaving Makal fuming in the back of the truck.

"The American?" Lem Sengor asked.

"Yeah. This changes everything," Makal muttered. "We're heading for the warehouse, and we're taking our cut now."

Sengor looked out the windshield, worry darkening his face. "But he's only after the Kongras, isn't he?"

"He's with the reporter. And he saw me," Makal replied. "He'll put two and two together about all of us. Even if he doesn't, we're mad dogs in his eyes."

Sengor winced. "Damn. I wish we'd never gotten involved in this crap."

"We're involved, like it or not," Makal answered.

"I just wanted to protect my city. Weeding out the Kong-ras while pretending to do them favors was one thing, but…" Sengor began.

"We'll take care of it."

"And what about Van?" Sengor asked, gesturing toward the wreckage around them. "We could be doing what we were recruited for!"

"Are you a paramedic?"

"No," Sengor answered.

"Does this jeep have a crane? Do we have search dogs?" Makal pressed.

"No! But those drugs could do a lot of good helping out the wounded," Sengor answered.

"They will. All of the supplies," Makal promised. "Except the stuff we can sell to boost our retirement fund."

Sengor frowned, keeping his eye on the cracked road.

"Trust me," Makal said. "We fill up the retirement fund, and then we pull apart Trug with what we know."

"What if Trug flips to save his ass?" Sengor asked.

Makal shook his head. "Trug's not going to even see a po-lice station let alone a jail cell."

Sengor's jaw tightened again.

"Trug's killed too many people for you to cry over if he gets a bullet in the head," Makal reminded him.

Sengor didn't say anything as he kept driving. Makal won-dered if everything was going to fall apart around him. If that was the case, then he wasn't going to sit still and let the pieces fall on his head.

BOLAN AND ABOOD DUCKED into a doorway as a troop truck raced past. Visible in the bed were several injured people, being tended to by tattered, shell-shocked soldiers.

"They're not too interested in finding us," Bolan surmised as he stepped out into the street.

"Lucky for us they're more interested in relief work than catching us," Abood mused.

"That's as it should be," Bolan said.

"Too bad it takes something like this to have people get their priorities straight."

Metal screeched and crashed in the distance. Bolan broke into a run, leaving Abood standing shocked for a moment before she spotted the truck jackknifed across the road. It was the transport that had just passed them. She took off after him, and the two reached the overturned vehicle in a moment.

"Are you okay?" Bolan asked one of the soldiers who had been thrown clear. Blood trickled down his cheek, and his eyes were unfocused. "Sit."

The soldier resisted for a heartbeat, but Bolan's strength guided him to the ground. "Cat."

"I'll talk to them," she answered.

"Good," Bolan replied. "I'll perform triage."

The bed of the truck was a mess. Stunned and injured people lay in a tangle of limbs. Someone in that mess shrieked in agony. Bolan reached in and started extricating the Turks, making certain that those who could walk stepped away from the truck.

He took a deep breath and smelled the pungent odor of spilled diesel fuel. The fuel was highly flammable, and he didn't know how long it would take to ignite the low-grade formula. One spark, and the truck could turn into a funeral pyre, the very nature of the diesel enabling it to burn far longer than a gasoline flame. Still, Bolan had to be cautious of handling the crash victims too roughly. Even before the truck turned over, many aboard were suffering from physical trauma.

Gently, he assisted the wounded to the street side.

"Cat! Tell them to clear back farther, there's diesel all over the place," Bolan called out.

Abood nodded and rushed to the gathered, stunned occupants of the truck.

Bolan saw the man who had been crying out in agony. His leg was twisted at an unnatural angle, and blood soaked into his pant leg just above his knee. The big American leaned in closer and the wounded man clutched his sleeve tightly, fingers digging like claws, even through the thick leather of his jacket and his blacksuit. He muttered something, but Bolan's grasp of Turkish wasn't enough to cut through the desperate words. He rested his hand on the wounded man's shoulder.

"Cat, I need a translator," Bolan called out.

A young man staggered into view. "This is my father. I can talk to him."

Abood looked nervously toward Bolan, but he shook his head and gestured for her to keep the crash victims back.

"Tell him that I have to stop the bleeding," Bolan said, "But it's going to hurt like hell."

The young man watched and spoke softly to his father as Bolan pulled off the wounded man's belt. The jagged end of a snapped bone stuck through the skin and muscle, and Bolan knew that as long as the bone poked through, it would hold the wound open.

"My father doesn't want to lose his leg," the young Turk said. "My name is Avi Malatya."

"I'll do my best. But right now…" Bolan drew the man's belt tightly around his thigh, just above the injury. The injured man screamed again, but choked it off as the pain subsided. "Help me drag him back farther."

The two of them managed to pull the wounded man thirty feet from the truck and Bolan knelt, undoing his improvised tourniquet. "I need a dressing."

Malatya tore off his own sleeve and wadded it. "Here."

"Thanks," Bolan replied as he placed the wad over the jutting bone. "Gently tug on his foot. We need to get that bone back beneath the skin."

"I'm in my second year of medical school. I came home for the holidays," Malatya replied.

"Good," Bolan said. He pulled out his wallet and stuck it in the man's teeth. Malatya was already telling his father to bite down hard. Bolan applied direct pressure as the son drew the leg out.

The pain had to have been horrendous, but the only outward signs the man showed were the muffled groans around the wallet. Once the leg was extended, and still holding the torn flesh closed with the improvised dressing, Bolan guided the bones back together. It was crude, battlefield first aid, but once they set the bone back in place, it wouldn't dislodge and cause more tissue damage. Pure luck had kept the jagged bone from severing the femoral artery.

"Get something to brace this with," Bolan said.

The student looked back toward the truck, then ran to the bed. Bolan almost cried out to stop him, but the boy was too quick. Fortunately, he didn't dally, finding four broken slats from a bench. As he rushed back, he took off his own belt.

"I'll hold the dressing, just cinch everything in place," Malatya said, applying his own weight to the dressing.

Bolan worked quickly, donating his own belt to the cause. The victim's belt was used to secure the dressing in place firmly, while the others secured the pieces of splint around the broken bone. By the time they were done, the injured man was pale and clammy. Still, he had enough presence of mind to spit out Bolan's wallet. Bite marks cut into the leather from his pain. He muttered something weakly.

"He thanks you," the medical student announced.

"I figured as much," Bolan answered.

"I saw the drivers in the cab. They weren't moving," the student told him. "Do you—"

"Stay here and help anyone else you can," Bolan replied. "I'll take care of them. You're better at this than I am."

"Not by much," the student answered, but the warrior was already halfway to the cab. As he reached the front of the truck, he looked past the fender. Diesel soaked the ground, and Bolan could see broken pipes sticking up. Wires sparked and sizzled from one of the pipes while another pumped sludgy fluids.

If one of those sparks touched the diesel fuel, it would be all over for the soldiers who crewed the truck. Bolan raced to the end of the spreading slick and took off his jacket. His guns would be obvious now, but under the circumstances, any difficulties he'd run into were insignificant compared to lives that needed saving. He used the jacket as a mop to push the growing puddle back, then stomped it into place to form a dam against the spilt fuel.

Bolan's nostrils informed him of the rotten-egg odor of natural gas. He turned, dread filling his gut. If the sparks ignited the natural gas, there was no telling how big the explosion would be. The student wandered around the fender nervously.

"What's wrong?"

"The gas main's cracked, and those wires are spitting like crazy," Bolan said. "Get everyone back."

The student rushed forward and kicked off his shoe. He frowned and clambered closer to the broken electrical conduit.

"Get—" Bolan began, but from a distance of five feet, Malatya tossed his shoe at the wires. The shoe clattered to one side, and the student started on his other foot. Bolan nodded at the logic and raced to grab the first shoe. The stench of natural gas—actually the chemical mixed in to alert people of the odorless mixture's potential leak—grew stronger. Bolan waved the student back, then gripping the rubber sole, he tugged it over the broken end of the pipe.

The wires would still spark but the shoe, with its heavy rubber and foam padding, would contain them, keeping them from igniting the leaking natural gas. Bolan rushed back to the cab.

The student was in midclimb to the door when Bolan waved him down. He drew the steel-framed Jericho and smashed a hole through the windshield with a hard snap of his wrist. He tugged the sleeves of his blacksuit down farther, gripped the hole in the glass and pulled forward. The rubber seal tore loose, and the glass screen came away in his shielded hands. The ripstop material resisted the jagged glass edges enough for Bolan to open a more direct route to save the two Turkish soldiers. The student leaned in, flicking open his pocketknife. He sawed one seat belt away and dragged the driver out into the open.

Bolan did the same for the other soldier, and the two of them brought the unconscious men to the rest of the group.

The student and Bolan compared notes.

"Concussions at least," Malatya said. "But no apparent neck injuries. Can't tell for sure unless we get them to a hospital."

"No wheels," Bolan replied.

"But I found a radio on the soldier you rescued," the student replied.

Bolan sighed with relief.

"I don't think you'll be sticking around, will you?" Malatya asked.

"What makes you think that?" Bolan asked.

"Your guns," the student concluded. He pulled off his baggy jacket. "See if you can fit into this."

Bolan tried, and while it was snug in the shoulders, it draped loosely enough to cover his guns. "Thanks."

"Get going. You look like you've got other things to worry about," Malatya said.

"What's your name?" Abood asked as she approached them.

"Avi," he said.

"Thanks for the help, Avi. And see about protecting that bare foot," Bolan warned.

"Just do what you have to do," Avi answered. "I'll worry about my feet when the cavalry arrives."

Bolan and Abood took that as their cue to leave, continuing their trek toward the warehouse.

10

"All right, let's split up. You see anything that could lead us to Abood and her mystery boyfriend, call me and I'll bring the boys running," Makal said to Sengor.

Sengor nodded, looking at the rubble-strewn streets. His mind was more on the catastrophe than finding their fugitives.

"Listen, if we find the drugs, we can help all those citizens you feel need it," Makal reminded him.

Sengor ran his fingers through his highlighted hair. The Turkish lawman frosted his normally dark hair to give him a more European look. It made him a little more attractive to women in the clubs, even though his partners razzed him about it. "Okay. If it's to help get the drugs back, except for what's going into our retirement funds—"

Makal rested his hand on Sengor's shoulder. "That's the spirit, blondie."

Sengor puffed out his jowls and took off.

Makal frowned as he watched his man leave, then checked the CZ-75 on his hip. He was going to need a deniable weapon in case he ran into Trug and his boys. Granted, Turkish forensics were a joke, but Makal was known for his big Czech pistol, a sign of how truly elite he was among the Jandarma. Most of the other paramilitary types still used postwar 9 mm Walther P-38s or Glocks. It wouldn't be hard for even a Turkish investigator to place the CZ-75's unique firing pin strike on spent brass, and Makal wasn't about to stick around to police his empties after emptying his gun into his Kongra-Gel co-conspirators.

He went to the back of his van and opened a case, setting down his gun and choosing a P-38. He inserted a full magazine, charged the chamber, then lowered the hammer with his thumb. For a cheap reload, he did the same with two more of the guns, tucking them farther out of sight under his jacket. Spare magazines went into his pockets, in case he'd have time to reload.

It wasn't a perfect plan, and he looked at the locked and cocked CZ lying alone in the case. He pursed his lips, then picked it back up and tucked it into his usual holster. He might need some high capacity if he got into real trouble. Makal also grabbed a collapsing stock G-3 and a bandolier of extra magazines. A quick check of the charge on his cell phone, and he was set.

LEM SENGOR CAME ACROSS the overturned truck as Turkish military units were helping the crash survivors. Major Baydur was talking with a young man wearing only one shoe, and Sengor jogged up to find out what was going on.

"Lem," Baydur spoke up, noticing him, "did you spot anything on Abood or the other man who attacked Makal?"

"Not a thing," Sengor said.

"They attacked Jandarma officers?" the one-shoed youth asked.

"The man did. He opened fire on them when they were questioning the woman. Catherine Abood," Baydur stated.

The youth frowned.

"You've seen them?" Sengor asked.

"They were the first ones here," the young man told them. "They helped rescue us, and did what they could to minimize the risk of the truck's fuel igniting."

Sengor tilted his head. "A tall man, black hair, dark skin, wearing some kind of commando outfit?"

"No. He was wearing normal clothes. A jacket, jeans, tight shirt," the youth replied.

"Which way did they go?" Baydur inquired.

The young man seemed to think about it for a moment, then pointed southeast. "They looked like they were cutting out of town. I don't think they wanted to hang around for any more aftershocks."

"Sounds like a smart plan," Baydur mused. "What do you think?"

Sengor's brow furrowed as he looked at the young man. "Yes. I can believe it. Only someone with a death wish would want to cross the city as it is."

"But something's bothering you," Baydur replied.

"They might try to circle around the city. Especially if they're involved with the Kongras," Sengor responded. "Try to find where the drugs are."

"You think they know where the relief supplies went?" Baydur asked.

"It's a possibility," Sengor told him. "I just don't know how."

"I don't care about how they're involved. If we ever needed relief supplies, now is the time," Baydur informed him. "Can you find them?"

Sengor outlined his plan. "I'm going to check with my informants. Go through the city, get a little bit ahead of them. If I do find out I'll call in backup."

"Do that," Baydur responded. "I could assign a team to work with you—"

"My informants might not like that," Sengor replied. "And your boys will only slow me down."

"In other words, you're going to get rough," Baydur translated.

Sengor shook his head. "Not like you're thinking."

"Makal has a reputation for skinning Kurdish separatists. And you're one of his elite team," Baydur replied.

"I've never hurt anyone who didn't have it coming," Sengor answered. "Besides, I'm half Kurd, or don't you read the files?"

"Yeah," Baydur answered. "I just… A lot of people don't like their families. Jews worked for Hitler. Palestinians assist the Mossad…"

"I'm not ashamed of my roots," Sengor answered.

Baydur looked at the blond tints streaking through Sengor's dark, upswept hair. "Right."

Sengor's face darkened and he sighed. "Just trust me, okay? We're trying to do good here."

Baydur studied him for a long time. "All right. But if Makal's behind anything rotten—"

"I'll tell you," Sengor stated. "In fact, I'll bring him in myself."

Sengor turned and headed out, working his way toward the warehouse, feeling Major Baydur's eyes boring holes in his back even after he'd turned the corner.

PEPIS AND BURSA WERE going over the maps, coordinating with the Ministry of the Interior and the Ministry of Defense. Van was in a bad way.

"Both highways from the south were destroyed. We can't get any trucks over them," Bursa said.

"Refugees have blocked the roads to the north," Pepis added. "With the roads to Mardin cut off, all we have is air transportation."

"It's going to be tight. The airport wasn't designed for much more than tourist traffic," Bursa lamented. "How's the situation in the surrounding countryside?"

"We're picking up aftershocks up to 3.9 as far away as

Kars," Pepis explained. "It's dropped in magnitude, but Van's being shaken like a chew toy."

Bursa looked at the map before him. The lines in blue and red gave him the ability to turn the catastrophe into an abstract, instead of the nightmare that threatened to invade his concentration. A ringing phone sliced through the dread slowly building at the bottom of his stomach, and he grabbed the receiver.

It was Cahil Gordi, the minister of defense.

"Tell me you have good news," Bursa said.

"We've got a nuclear aircraft carrier from the Americans. It's coming in full steam and is going to park in the Gulf of Iskenderun," Gordi told him.

"That'll be a four-hundred-mile flight, both ways," Bursa answered.

"It's still aircraft. The British and Italians are also sending relief ships."

"How soon will all of this be in place?" Bursa asked.

Gordi paused. "The carrier will pull in tonight, around eight."

Bursa closed his eyes. He did the math. Even if their helicopters raced full-out at top speed, it was going to be more than two hours for them to send in supplies and emergency response teams. Add time for dispersal through the city, and it would be well after midnight before the Americans could lend a hand.

In the meantime, people needed help immediately. "It's going to take too long," Bursa murmured.

"The carrier has AWACS aircraft en route over the area," Gordi said, hope tingeing his voice.

"Their radar planes?" Bursa inquired.

"They can do much more than just keep track of planes and ships," Gordi explained. "Sure, they can identify aircraft two hundred nautical miles away, but they are also forward command and control centers."

"Communications," Bursa mused, his spirits starting to lift.

"Communications, and forward air traffic control for our own planes. Van's airports are down. Power outages and damage have knocked out their radar and communications for now. One AWACS can guide relief aircraft in to give aid," Gordi told him.

"Thank God." Bursa sighed with relief. He looked over to Pepis.

The seismologist frowned as he looked at the readings coming in.

"What's wrong?" Bursa inquired.

"We've got a buildup coming," Pepis said. He pointed to three locations on the map. "Tremors in Elazio and Diyarbakir are building up. Faults in their area are starting to loosen up in sympathy with the main quake that hit Van."

Bursa's brow furrowed. "Are they…"

"It's hard to tell how much pressure those faults have built up for now. But even if they release at less than 4.0…" Pepis began. The seismologist stepped away from the map. "Even if they release with a minimum of force, it's going to send shock waves rolling back into Van."

"Destabilizing things further," Bursa concluded, lowering the phone. "Damn."

Pepis rubbed his forehead. "The shock waves might null out in the center, but waves can reflect off each other. It's simple physics."

"And the shock waves will roll back into Van," Bursa grumbled.

"The city has been hit hard. I'll be surprised if any buildings are still standing now," Pepis told him. "The aftershocks are only making things worse."

"I'll tell the minister," Bursa said, leaving Pepis alone.

Mack Bolan caught the flash of light reflecting on a gun barrel just in time and he whirled, scooping Abood off her feet and hurling them both behind a pile of rubble. A rifle shot smashed into the crushed mound, spraying stone chips and dust everywhere. Dumping Abood on the sidewalk and behind cover, he whipped out his weapon, leveling it in the direction where the gunfire came from.

He froze.

The figure holding the rifle was small, a child of twelve or so. Whipping to one side, Bolan avoided a second gunshot and holstered his pistol.

As if the Executioner couldn't have guessed the kid's intent, she shouted in Turkish, "Stay away!"

"Cat! Try to talk to her!" Bolan said.

Abood poked her head up and another gunshot exploded.

Black hair flew in a cloud of black silk. Bolan's gut dropped, and he started toward her. Another round struck the street in front of him, and he swerved out of the way. Bolan dropped into a crouch the second he reached the corner of one of the two buildings bracketing the rifle-armed girl. The USP Compact was in his hand again.

"Cat?"

"Fuck," he heard her snarl.

Bolan's grip relaxed on the polymer grip of the pistol. "You okay?"

"I got shot in the head," Abood grumbled. He saw her shift her position. She had her Beretta out, ready to continue the battle.

"Hold off and keep down," Bolan told her. "It's just a kid."

Three rounds exploded rapidly against the brick at Bolan's shoulder, and he took a step out of the way. Whatever the kid's fight was, she was armed to the teeth from the sound of it. The chugging booms of her rifle were indicative of an AK.

But the girl had either patience only to fire single shots, or she didn't know how to flick the selector lever on the big gun to full-auto. Either way, she'd have more than enough power to hold off the Executioner in the confines of the alley.

Bolan looked along the storefront. The large picture window to his side was destroyed, leaving gaps large enough for him to wriggle through. He peeked around the window frame, and was rewarded with the snap of a handgun. Glass shattered and Bolan hit the ground.

"That way's no good," Bolan murmured. "Cat?"

"I'm fine," Abood shouted back. "Whatever hit me just split the skin on my forehead!"

Bolan grimaced. "How badly?"

"Enough that I can't see out of my right eye for all the blood. What about you?" Abood asked.

"I've got another shooter inside the storefront," Bolan explained.

"They've made it fairly obvious that they don't want us around," Abood replied.

"Talk to them. Let them know we mean them no harm," Bolan told her. "Otherwise, they're not going to let us retreat in peace."

"Retreat?" Abood asked.

"I don't have the time to throw these kids over my knee.

And I don't have the inclination, either. They're protecting their home!" Bolan stated.

Abood took an audible breath and spoke up in Turkish.

The girl in the alley fired a shot at the pile of rubble that the journalist had taken cover behind.

"Damn it!" Abood growled and she scurried away from her position.

"Don't shoot them!" Bolan ordered.

Abood shouted something. It didn't sound very friendly, but it was in Turkish. If she had cursed the girl, Bolan wouldn't know.

The rifle-toting Turkish girl snapped out a bitter-sounding response. But, this time, no thundering gunfire accompanied it. An even younger-sounding boy spoke inside of the storefront.

"Crap, the other kid told Annie Oakley not to believe us," Abood announced. "He said you're trying to sneak in behind her."

Bolan shook his head. That had been his intent, but he was going to try to disarm the girl, not shoot her in the back.

"What's the deal?" Abood asked.

"Let them know we're not looters," Bolan called back. "We only want to help."

Abood translated for Bolan and he raised his obviously empty hands above the sill. Glass smashed as a bullet launched, but the Executioner didn't flinch. Even though the boy was armed, he hadn't displayed any great skill as a marksman, as opposed to the girl Bolan assumed was his sister.

The girl spoke up, the boy chiming in. For a desperate moment, the siblings argued.

Bolan raised his head above the sill.

The younger brother cracked off another shot. It was two feet wide of the Executioner, shattering more glass.

The boy looked to be around nine years old, and he held

what looked like a .45 in his shaking hands. Bolan rose and knew that the youngster wasn't going to have trouble putting a bullet into his chest given the mechanical accuracy of the weapon. But he was still at the warning-shot stage.

The boy shouted at him, motioning with the muzzle.

"Cat…"

Abood was talking fast now. She'd stepped out from behind the rubble, her gun hidden under her photographer's vest. From the corner of his eye, Bolan could see that the right side of her face was smeared in blood. Her hands were empty.

The girl hadn't fired another shot since the negotiations began.

The boy triggered his weapon. This shot whizzed high, blasting glass at the top of the window. Bolan only turned his head aside enough to avoid splinters in his face.

Abood's hand dropped to her side, but she resisted the urge to draw her Beretta. Half blind and standing in the middle of the street, she'd have been easy prey for the rifle-armed girl.

Except for the boy, everyone had held their fire in this bit of excitement.

The girl appeared at the opening of the walkway. The rifle looked almost too heavy for her to hold, but she kept its muzzle aimed at Bolan. He nodded, acknowledging her presence, his hands still up and in view.

The girl spoke.

"She wants to know whose side you're on," Abood translated.

"Tell her that we're on her side."

The girl stabbed the rifle muzzle at Bolan, like a spear, her dark face hard and stern as she spoke again.

"She wants to know if we're Jandarma."

Bolan shook his head. "No."

The girl spoke again, understanding the universal term. Abood did her best to keep up with her.

"She says that she's afraid for her brother. Not the one in the store. Her older brother. The Jandarma picked him up just before the earthquake hit," Abood said. "He's all that they had after their parents were executed for being in the PKK."

The Kurdish People's Party, Bolan knew, had been reduced to outlaw status because of actions its members took to fight organized racism on governmental levels. The Jandarma had done a good job of rounding up suspected members, and anyone who resisted was killed. Kangaroo trials were the order of the day. The Kongra-Gel was an evolution of the PKK, though neither side could be considered saintly.

"The Jandarma is after us too, remember?" Bolan asked.

Abood explained their situation quickly.

The girl looked doubtful, but the nose of her AK dropped to the ground. She leaned against the wall, in relief that she didn't have to hold up the heavy weapon. She called the boy's name—Kandor—and shouted what sounded like an order.

Kandor snapped back angrily. Bolan's Turkish hadn't improved, but he could translate on tone alone. "You're not the boss of me," was what modern American kids would have replied.

Bolan dredged up a phrase in Turkish. "Please?"

The boy looked at him. He spoke rapidly to Bolan, but the Executioner shook his head, recalling another crash-course phrase he remembered. "I only speak a little Turkish."

Kandor paused, then lowered his handgun. The boy jogged out front.

Kandor and his sister sneered at each other, and Abood interrupted them with a few stern words.

Bolan turned his gaze up and down the street, looking for more trouble.

A jeep whirled around the corner. Its top was down, and grim, angry men with rifles rode inside. It didn't take much imagination to guess who they were.

Bolan scooped up Kandor in one smooth movement. "Jandarma!"

Abood grabbed the sister and her rifle and the four of them bolted through the store's door as the jeep rolled at them.

Abood's head ducked through the doorway just before a rifle slug blasted the molding she'd ducked behind. Bolan whipped up his pistol and triggered two quick shots. The 9 mm slugs leaped through the shattered window and struck the hood of the jeep.

The Jandarma driver swerved, throwing off the aim of his partners, buying the Executioner precious seconds.

"I think you only made them angry," Abood stated as she grabbed the girl by her arm and dragged her inside.

Bolan steered them behind the counter and into a doorway to a back room. A stairwell led to the next floor, but the top was blocked with tossed furniture. Bolan pushed Kandor onto the steps, then moved to allow Abood to take his sister up.

Abood paused, then asked the girl something. "Ro says you can take the rifle."

Bolan smiled and accepted the offering, and a spare magazine. "Tell her I'll get it back to her."

Abood nodded and hurried up the stairwell.

The Executioner moved away from the stairwell and took cover at the counter.

The three Jandarma riflemen came through the door, their weapons spitting lead. Heavy-caliber slugs tore through the wood of the counter and punched into the wall behind it. Had Bolan not pressed flat to the floor, he'd have been torn to shreds. Instead, he stayed put, pulling out the powerful Jericho.

There was a long silence before he saw shadows fall across the holes torn by rifle bullets in the counter. Bolan fired at the shadowed holes, his .40-caliber cannon tearing through the counter. A scream of agony split the air and a body fell to the floor. Scrambling boots resounded, and Bolan took the opportunity to somersault out from behind the counter.

The AK was held in one fist, like a handgun. The Executioner wouldn't have precision control over the weapon, but on single shot, he was able to fill the air with high-powered lead.

One of the fleeing Jandarma thugs whirled and opened fire, but the spray of slugs from his weapon flew into the ceiling as Bolan's retaliation caught him in the chest. The rifleman slammed against the doorjamb, then slid slowly to the ground. The other gunman escaped out the door and rushed toward the jeep.

The driver pulled up a shotgun from a sidesaddle sheath just above the bumper. He shouted angrily, but Bolan swung on him. The driver and his weapon disappeared beneath the dashboard as slugs sparked on the steel fender of the jeep. Bolan had held his fire on the Jandarma soldiers as long as possible, but their decision to open fire on a group that included children justified his reaction. They didn't care if kids got caught in their cross fire.

That was enough to assuage any guilt the Executioner would have harbored in returning fire. The AK locked empty, and Bolan let it hang on its sling.

The driver, hearing the rifle fire come to an end, popped up with his shotgun. He rose right in front of the muzzle of Bolan's Jericho and caught two high-powered slugs in the chest. The shotgunner spit up a gout of blood as the Executioner's .40-caliber bullets smashed through his ribs and tore his lungs and heart to a pulp. The corpse slid out of the driver's seat and into the street.

The last standing gunman reloaded his rifle and poked its muzzle around the window. He fired blindly, the weapon's muzzle-flash lighting up the store. His shots sliced at chest height, but Bolan was still crouched, staying out of the way of the slaughtering salvo. He took the opportunity to load a fresh magazine into his AK. He left the selector on single shot and was working across the floor when the first gunman grabbed his leg.

Bolan stumbled as the wounded Jandarma thug yanked his foot out from under him. Crashing to the floor, his AK clattered halfway to the door. The rifleman outside paused in his shooting, but Bolan knew he had a more immediate threat as the wounded gunman rose from playing possum. One bloodied hand struggled to reach for a handgun in its holster, the flap not responding to his blood-slicked fingers.

The Executioner braced himself on his hands and snapped a hard kick across the injured man's jaw. The Turk's head bounced violently backward, and he collapsed to the floor. Bolan wasn't going to give him a chance to recover, so he swung around and yanked the stunned killer off the ground.

With a violent twist, Bolan brought the dazed rifleman between him and the vigilante in the doorway. Rifle bullets struck the stunned man's back, and the Executioner shoved the dying thug along, using him as a shield. Bolan and the corpse in his grasp hammered into the other Jandarma killer, jarring his weapon from his grasp. All three crashed out of the doorway and into the street.

The remaining Jandarma marauder reached for the handgun in his holster while he pushed at Bolan with his free hand. The Executioner wanted to know the condition of Kandor and Ro's older brother, and if he could be rescued, so he gripped the Turk's forearm and punched him hard in the elbow. Bone snapped and the joint cracked apart with a crunch, stopping the man's fumbling fast draw. Bolan twisted the broken limb hard and pushed his adversary face-first into the sidewalk. As the Turk gargled in pain, the Executioner retrieved the thug's handgun and G-3 rifle.

"Cat? You okay?" he called out.

"Yeah," Abood said. She came out from behind the counter. The kids stayed put, under her orders.

"I need to find out from this guy where Kandor and Ro's older brother is," Bolan told her.

Abood knelt and, drawing her Beretta, ground the muzzle into the captive's temple. She spoke quickly in Turkish, her tone matching the ugly sound of the Turkish words leaving her lips. She looked up at Bolan when the Jandarma enforcer refused to answer.

"Give him a twist," she said.

Bolan wrenched the wounded man's forearm. Tears and screams escaped the injured thug, and he began sputtering for mercy.

Abood cocked the hammer on her handgun and continued to grill the man.

He spoke, spittle flying from his lips, mucus running from his nose. The Turk had lost it, completely. Pain and fear combined to make him putty in their hands.

"He's being held a mile and a half that way," Abood noted. "The Jandarma have set up a command post, and have been rounding up suspected Kongra-Gel sympathizers."

"Is their brother okay?" Bolan asked.

"They've administered beatings. The commander, Makal, sent this crew over here to pick up the kids, or their corpses, to give them leverage against the older brother," Abood explained.

Bolan looked down in disgust at his prisoner. Had he been someone given to pure and simple vengeance, he'd have continued twisting the jackbooted thug's arm off. Instead, he let go and flipped him over onto his back with a sweep of his boot. The Jandarma man gibbered in fear.

"He wants to know what you're going to do," Abood translated.

"We're going to take your guns, your jeep and the children.

You are going to disappear," Bolan told him. "How you disappear depends on whether you try to warn your commander."

Abood translated and the man swallowed visibly. Terror widened his dark eyes.

"He says he'll behave," she told Bolan.

"I'm going to tie him up," Bolan explained.

Abood translated. The man was frightened, but more than a little relieved.

"Rescuing the brother—"

"It'll take some time out, and it'll be a risk," Bolan agreed. "But do you want to leave their only remaining family at the mercy of these mad dogs?"

"Hell no," Abood answered. "I just wanted to make sure you were willing to get sidetracked again."

"Willing to get sidetracked?" Bolan plucked the Jandarma thug's handgun from its holster. "Yeah."

The doomsday numbers ticked down, not just for the medical supplies, but for the older brother.

12

Aydin Zeki coughed, blood pouring from a cut inside his cheek. He could still breathe, and stand. They were going easy on him, and he knew why.

It was because Makal hadn't arrived yet. Instead, Lem Sengor arrived at the improvised Jandarma command post, and looked with sullen eyes at the pack of prisoners the Jandarma crew had picked up.

"Please," Sengor said, "make it easy on yourself. Just tell them what you've heard. Tell them anything."

Zeki looked at him, one of his eyes swollen half shut from the beating. "Even if I knew lies, I wouldn't tell them."

Sengor pinched the flesh between his own eyebrows, blinking away exhaustion. This had been too long a day, and it was barely noon. He'd been up all evening, working with Makal on corralling Abood's informant. And then, that stupid witch sneaked in the back, killing the kid and shooting Gogin. The hairs at the back of his neck bristled.

Makal had thrown a tarp over the kid, and as much as he wanted to believe that Recep Arcuri was part of Kagan Trug's effort to screw them all over, the way the cloth stuck to the young man's corpse in so many places…

Sengor had seen that kind of a mess only a few times before. When Makal and Gogin had finished a grueling peeling session, when they'd strip the flesh from a prisoner, demanding an answer or else strips of flesh were torn off. Most of the time, those interrogated spoke after the first inch-wide section of skin was torn off. They left, bleeding through their shirts, missing one inch-wide, twelve-inch ribbon of skin, providing several answers to what Makal needed. Once broken, those people became ready sources of information for Makal's strike team.

Others had either nothing to say, or the will to keep quiet. They were few and far between. And when Makal was finished, their corpses were wrapped in blood-soaked tarps, skinned muscle sticking to cloth.

"Makal's on the warpath, Aydin," Sengor told the young man. "If you don't have anything for him, he'll tear the hide off you like an orange peel."

Zeki's lip twitched. "And it'll end with a bullet in my head. Then I'll get to see my parents."

Sengor brushed his fingers through his stiff, blond-frosted hair. He paced the tent once, twice, then glared at Zeki. "What about Ro and Kandor?"

Zeki's lips tightened into a bloodless line.

"Who's going to take care of your brother and sister?" Sengor pressed. "Please. One name. One address. Anything you might know about the missing medical supplies. And they can have an older brother, someone who can watch over them."

Zeki's eyes softened as he thought about his siblings. That gave Sengor a measure of hope. He hated when things got rough with kids. Zeki wasn't even eighteen. And with two preteen siblings to care for, his torture and execution would leave two more orphans, hungry and hating the world.

Sengor leaned in close. "Talk to me. I can make Makal lay off."

Zeki took a deep breath. "Boz Arcuri was in on the theft. And he's angry."

"Boz? Who's he after?" Sengor asked. His mind flashed back to Recep's corpse, covered with the tarp. Sick dread wrenched in his gut.

"The American," Zeki replied. "The American and that bitch who seduced Recep into betraying the Kongras. They're going to pay for flaying Recep."

Sengor stepped back. "Do you know where any of them are?"

Zeki shook his head. "Just that Arcuri is going to tear his way through Van. If you're between him and them, that's it."

Sengor rubbed his jaw, mind racing at the implications. He squeezed his guilt back down into his gut and nodded. "All right. I'll see what kind of a deal I can cut with the local commander."

Zeki sighed, shoulders sagging.

"Nah. No deals, Sengor," came the unbidden answer. Lieutenant Erdogan came in, hand on the butt of his gun. "I'm sick of you turning easy on us."

Sengor's jaw clenched. "You know what you need to."

"The kid knows more. And we're going to get it out of him," Erdogan explained. Three of the Jandarma commander's men swarmed into the tiny tent. One of them leveled a Walther at a spot above Sengor's navel. "If the bastard makes a move, kill him."

Lem Sengor's shoulders tensed as he watched Erdogan drag Zeki out of his chair.

MACK BOLAN LOWERED HIS monocular and slipped it back into his combat harness. He lifted the G-3 and clicked the selector to full-auto, then waved for Abood to start the jeep. Kandor and Ro were in the vehicle with her. It was a risky proposition bringing the kids so close to the conflict, but the Executioner didn't want the young people scattered halfway across the city. When he grabbed Aydin Zeki and rescued him, he wanted the family back together immediately.

And they'd need the jeep to hightail it out of town.

The wire folding stock was locked in place. Spare magazines, "donated" by the Jandarma, were stuffed in magazine pouches, also from the same source.

But things had gotten complicated. The commander of the local unit had grabbed Zeki, and was holding another Jandarma at gunpoint.

The way the one under the gun acted, there was little doubt in Bolan's mind that this guy with the blond highlights was opposed to whatever tactics the squad leader was about to engage in.

Bolan knew he wouldn't have long to rescue Zeki, and now he was going to add the Jandarma man with a conscience to his list of tagalongs. Guns at the ready, his Heckler & Koch full of borrowed 9 mm ammunition, the Jericho in reserve in case he needed a powerful, single bullet or a quick reload, the Executioner was in war mode.

Abood gunned the engine and raced past the front of the improvised camp. Ro fired a burst of autofire into the sky as they tore away.

That got the Jandarma's attention.

A dozen armed men rushed out into the street. Bolan slipped around the back, cutting through the rubble that used to be a building and approaching the open lot the Jandarma thugs were using as their impromptu prison camp. By the time the Turkish hard force was in its own vehicles to give chase, Abood would have developed a strong lead. Enough to dangle herself as bait to encourage their pursuit, but far enough ahead that she could quickly lose them.

Three jeeps pulled out, leaving a handful of guards behind for the scraggly lot of Kongra-Gel suspects. Bolan had counted on that reaction, and the Jandarma commander was frozen, out in the open. Aydin Zeki was gripped between two burly thugs, and the blond Jandarma cop was still under the watchful gun of a third of the commander's men.

Bolan shouldered his rifle, thumbed the selector back to single shot, and fired through the mesh window of the tent. The single report caused the Jandarma lieutenant to whirl, his brutish goons reacting a moment later.

But that gave the blond Turk an opportunity to act.

THE BULLET SMASHED through the Jandarma gunman's shoulder, and Lem Sengor acted swiftly. The Walther hadn't even slipped from the guard's grasp when the brawny Turk punched the bullet wound and pried the pistol free.

Sengor shoved the guard aside and burst out of the tent. From atop the mountain of rubble that used to be a building, a tall man with a rifle leveled his weapon at Erdogan and his flunkies, shouting for them to drop their weapons and release Aydin Zeki.

Other guards spun and opened fire on Bolan, but he ducked out of the way, skidding down the flat slope of a fallen wall. Single shots punched the concrete at the guards' feet, driving them back.

It didn't take too much for Sengor to realize that the mysterious newcomer was out to help the prisoners, and had given Sengor an opportunity to escape. The man grabbed Zeki and pulled him from between Erdogan's hulks. One swung a trunklike arm at Sengor, but the half-Kurdish Jandarma member punched the barrel of the Walther under the man's ribs, knocking the wind from him.

Zeki kicked the other thug in the groin, but the boy still wasn't free. Sengor cracked the frame of the Walther along the hulk's cheek, but he ignored even that impact.

Erdogan went for his pistol, intending to gun down Aydin and Sengor while they were still occupied. Sengor snaked around the bulk of the huge Jandarma goon and pulled the trigger on his Walther, firing three shots into Erdogan's chest. Those bullets sprouted wounds at the same time as a burst of rifle rounds nearly tore the skull off Erdogan's shoulders.

The hulk still holding Zeki rammed his elbow into Sengor's shoulder, hurling him to the ground.

The other guards were uncertain what to do. The wraith on the rubble was too swift for them to shoot, and yet he fired deliberately at their feet, driving them back, calling for them to drop their guns and leave.

Bolan knew that his gambit was wearing thin. The rattle of gunfire would attract the attention of the pursuit party, and both Zeki and Sengor were still at the mercy of Erdogan's burly subordinate. While the huge goon hadn't resorted to lethal force, and could only have been following orders, Bolan was reluctant to shoot someone who might not have been directly involved in torture and murder.

Aydin Zeki acted, snaking his legs and tangling them with the huge Jandarma thug's. Sengor kicked up hard, catching the hulk in the crotch. Scrotum mashed, and with all the strength in Sengor's legs upsetting the entangled Jandarma giant's balance, he toppled to the concrete.

Sengor sat up, then looked at Bolan. The two of them held each other's gaze for what felt like an eternity, but a moment later, Sengor turned to the other guards.

"Drop your weapons!" Sengor ordered. "This man is from Interpol! He's been assisting in an investigation!"

The guards looked confused.

"Lieutenant Erdogan sold you out to Kagan Trug," Sengor continued, making up his story as he went along. "He was in on the theft of the medical supplies. When Captain Makal had me come to interrogate him, he took me at gunpoint!"

Bolan closed with Sengor and Zeki. The Executioner leveled the muzzle of his rifle at the ground at his side.

The two hulks stirred to uneasy alertness and crawled away from the site of the brawl. Sengor turned and hoped that the newcomer spoke English.

"Quick, give me a name," Sengor told him.

"Brandon Stone," Bolan answered quickly.

"Lem Sengor," the Jandarma man returned in a rushed whisper. He switched swiftly to Turkish. "This is Inspector Stone. He's an American."

Bolan made out his cover name, the term "inspector" and "American," and figured that Sengor was concocting a quick cover story for them. He stood beside Zeki and the Jandarma man, and made a visible point of flicking his rifle to safe.

He waited for Sengor to answer any challenges from the Jandarma.

"What about the prisoners?" an officer asked, stepping forward. "How come you were speaking with them?"

Sengor nodded. "Erdogan wanted these people rounded up because a few of them might have been able to implicate him. Aydin, he'd seen Erdogan talking with Arcuri."

Zeki nodded in agreement, going along with the scam.

"The others, they were just on a list of usual suspects that Erdogan could round up. With a large enough group, who'd notice one or two witnesses dead?" Sengor explained.

Bolan stood, hiding the uneasiness crawling up his spine. He didn't understand completely what was going on, or what Sengor was spinning for his fellow Jandarma thugs.

The three jeeps that had pulled out in pursuit of Abood roared into the entrance of the impromptu prison, the Jandarma hardmen inside confused about what had happened. They saw Lieutenant Erdogan, decapitated by gunfire.

The guards who had stayed behind caught the newcomers up to speed, leaving Bolan and his two charges standing unmolested. They were easy targets, and if someone thought

Sengor's story stunk, one pull of the trigger would drop three more corpses on the grounds of the camp.

Bolan remained alert.

One of Erdogan's men walked over to the corpse.

The guard in the tent groaned painfully, drawing the man's attention.

Bolan's face was impassive as Sengor continued to weave his tale, this time it spun easier as he had the truth to work from.

"Erdogan ordered him to shoot me if I tried to stop them from killing this boy," Sengor explained. "Inspector Stone shot only to wound. I disarmed him and went after Erdogan."

The wounded man was too groggy to answer coherently. Blood loss was setting in.

"Well, help him out!" Sengor ordered.

The Jandarma hard force rushed to the injured man's side.

"Are they buying it?" Bolan asked.

"Looks like it," Sengor replied. He looked Bolan over, realization dogging at his mind. "You're the one who rescued Abood, right?"

Bolan nodded.

"And shot four other Jandarma operatives," Sengor stated.

The tension in the air started to strain the situation. Their truce was fragile enough. The anger in the Turk's face showed that splinters were breaking off the brittle, temporary understanding.

"I gave those men the opportunity to back off."

Sengor looked at the pile of rubble that Bolan had come off. The Executioner was acutely aware of the muzzle of the Walther as it tracked toward his stomach. If Sengor pulled the trigger, there wouldn't be a single defensible way that he could stop the Turk. Luckily, Sengor's trigger finger rested on the frame.

"He was going to have his men rape the reporter," Sengor prodded.

"And they reacted badly to my telling them to back off," Bolan explained. "They fired first."

Sengor's face screwed up angrily, but the Walther muzzle pointed at the ground. Thick fingers raked through his frosted hair, and he took a step away from Bolan. The other Jandarma looked at the blond Turk, and Sengor shook his head.

"He lost contact with someone else in on the heist," Sengor explained. He turned back to Bolan and quickly translated the story he'd concocted for the others.

"That should work," Bolan answered. "You know Captain Makal?"

"I'm part of his team," Sengor replied. "He's my immediate superior."

Bolan waited a moment, not saying a word.

Sengor brushed his fingers across his hooked nose. "Not everyone working for Makal is willing to cut up kids. Did Abood say what Makal did to Recep?"

"Stripped the skin off him. She tried to get him away from Makal and his partner, but instead, Recep caught a bullet," Bolan stated.

Sengor grit his teeth. "That bastard told me that Abood put a slug in Recep, and Makal's partner, Gogin."

Bolan nodded.

"Oh, and I think that you've got Boz Arcuri on your tail," Sengor told him.

Bolan remembered what spotty intel he had on the Kongra-Gel. "Arcuri is Kagan Trug's top enforcer, isn't he?"

Sengor nodded. "And supposedly, he's the guy who triggered the blast that killed the relief workers."

Bolan took a deep breath. "So he's blaming me for what happened to Recep?"

"You or Abood. But he's definitely on the lookout for you," Sengor stated.

"Well, neither of us did that. It was Makal," Bolan explained. "But that doesn't let Arcuri off the hook. He's as much a mad-dog killer as anyone."

Sengor nodded. "Makal was in on the theft, but, I can't say anything right here."

"Because you're a part of it too?" Bolan asked.

Sengor's face tightened with guilt. "It was supposed to be a robbery. We'd skim enough off the top to set up our retirement funds, and then snap on Trug when he tries to move the product out of the country."

Bolan nodded. "Makal told you that you were cozying up to Trug in order to get the goods on him."

Sengor agreed with a nod, his face still in a mask of pain and dread. "I think Trug used Makal's unit as a bogeyman. We were the ones that came down the hardest on the Kongras and former PKK members. And Makal…"

"He'd skin a few people to get the information he wanted, or needed."

"I'd been on hand for a few sessions of rough stuff, but usually with real suspects, ones we're sure have killed people. You might understand what I'm saying."

Bolan nodded, knowing that Sengor understood what he was attempting to do. "I understand. Sometimes, you have to be a little outlaw to do the right thing," he said.

"But not killing kids," Sengor replied. "And not killing anyone who isn't guilty. I joined the strike team to take action against murderers."

"I know. And you've had some trouble. Any more Jandarma on Makal's case?"

"Our top commander for the region. Baydur. He's trying to reform things. He has his suspicions about Makal and the team. And me," Sengor said. "But he thinks he can turn me to the straight and narrow."

"Only if you want to go there," Bolan replied.

"I do," Sengor answered. "This business is making me sick."

"I'll help," Bolan told him. "But I'll need you to help me more."

"And Abood?" Sengor asked.

"She's taking the kids to a secure location. We're going to meet up with them," Bolan explained. "Get a jeep for us. And we'll take Aydin too."

Zeki reacted to the sound of his name, and Sengor had to switch gears.

"It's okay, Aydin. Inspector Stone knows where Kandor and Ro are," Sengor explained.

"Okay," Aydin replied, uncertain.

"He'll take us to them, and I'm going to make sure that no one else leans on you," Sengor promised.

"Were you really investigating?"

"Yes," Sengor said. "Don't even think that we weren't."

Zeki nodded and kept quiet.

Sengor smiled and winked.

"We'll need a ride out of here," Bolan said. "I was going to snag my own set of wheels—"

"I'll get them," Sengor said. He moved off to speak with the other Jandarma soldiers as they started to release their prisoners. His heart didn't weigh as heavily as he did so.

Lem Sengor saw the light at the end of this damned tunnel he'd been railroaded into.

CAT ABOOD WAS GLAD to see the Jandarma jeeps peel off, leaving her with Kandor and Ro, driving alone through the rubble-strewn streets of Van. Her AK-47 rested between the bucket seats, muzzle pointing upward. Ro held on to her old rifle, having proved her own skill with the weapon. Kandor sat in the back seat, unarmed, but looking relieved that he didn't have to fight.

Abood attributed that relief to the fact that the boy knew, deep down, that he was a lousy shot. She remembered being that young, and having first taken shots with a Glock her father had given to her. The recoil was frightening and she couldn't hit the broad side of a barn. She did much better with the .22 her dad gave her. Kandor would just have to bulk up a little, and get some actual training to feel comfortable shooting guns again.

Abood swerved around another corner and slowed down so as not to wreck the suspension of the jeep. She reminded herself that it was her duty to keep the kids safe and sound, so that Kandor could grow up.

Abood kept her eyes open for trouble, as did Ro.

Stone's plan was to set up a rendezvous, far enough from the improvised prison camp that the mysterious soldier could bring back Aydin with no problem, and they wouldn't be separated for long if she heard the sounds of a major battle. A few cracks of rifle fire resounded in the distance, and while Abood expected the worst, she knew that the big man in black wasn't going to go down with as little gunfire as that. She parked the jeep behind a pile of rubble and waited.

The gunfire ended quickly, but Abood's nerves were still on edge. Something was hovering, just outside her conscious perception. She didn't call it intuition, or a sixth sense. It was something that her subconscious mind picked up. Her father had written about that phenomena among veteran cops.

Maybe she'd spent enough time in dirty holes like this country to pick up on bad vibes, she thought.

"Take cover. If there's any trouble, don't move. I think we're being watched," Abood told Ro.

"But if you leave…"

"Stone and Aydin will find you. This is where we agreed to come," Abood told her. "It'll be fine. Just tell Stone that I was drawing away unwanted company."

Ro's dark eyes widened, and her lips pursed tightly.

"You've got your rifle," Abood said. "Just hole up, stay put and fend off anyone who stays behind."

Ro nodded and she grabbed Kandor by the hand. He looked reluctant to go, but Abood handed the boy a rifle. "Make sure you keep it on single shot."

Kandor held the ten-pound rifle, cradling it across both his arms. The boy seemed a little more confident.

"It won't hurt to shoot as much as the handgun did," she added, and Kandor smiled.

The kids scrambled away from the jeep and scurried into the front door of the building. Stone and Abood had checked it out earlier. It was their fallback position. The structure was still sound, and the front hallway was the only one that needed to be defended. Two children with rifles might hold off an army if necessary.

Abood hoped it wouldn't come to that, and she started the engine. She pulled away from the building, slowly. Some instinct told her that the predator that stalked her didn't want the children.

Amid the tremors, rubble and destruction, she could feel the palpable hate focused on her, like the rays of the sun on an ant, through a magnifying glass—hot, tight, burning anger like she'd never known before. She made sure the AK was still secure.

Over the sound of her own engine, she heard the sudden roar of another jeep. She glanced in the side mirror and saw a boxy shape shoot out of an alley. She gunned the engine and swerved as the vehicle clipped her fender. Abood held on, steering into her spin, and came out on the other end to see the enemy jeep several yards away. Shaken, she still managed to tromp on the gas and charge toward the hunter's vehicle. He was alone, and he struggled to steer into a head-on collision with her, but she hauled up the AK and fired a burst.

The heavy rifle suppressed the recoil, but not enough to

keep most of her shots on target. Metal sparked where she did connect, but the rest of the slugs sailed over the top of the jeep. The attacking driver had ducked behind the dashboard, out of her line of fire. She caught a glimpse of the hunter's face out of the corner of her eye.

It was livid with rage, lips peeled back into a rictus of hatred. Abood wrenched the jeep around a corner, hearing the clatter of rifle fire off the rear of the jeep. If Kandor and Ro had still been sitting in the jeep with her, they would have been torn apart, holes ripped through the back of the shotgun seat.

Abood's instincts were still sharp. She swung away from a chunk of rubble that would have folded the jeep in on itself, and hit the brakes. It left her open for a moment, but she wondered if her pursuer would end up running into a wall. She clambered out of the vehicle as the hunter's jeep tore around the corner at full speed.

Abood had just ducked behind the massive chunk of broken concrete when she heard brakes squeal in protest. The slab she hid behind shifted several inches, digging up road, and she backed away from the impact. Her hunter had played right into her trap.

Abood swung around, confidence and urgency prodding her. Something tingled at the base of her spine, something wrong, and she paused, half-exposed over the top of the fallen masonry. In the distance, she spotted a figure scrambling in the road. The jeep, crumpled against the fallen section of building, smoldered, but it was empty.

The woman tried to dive back behind cover when a blast of gunfire sounded in the air. Something hot speared into her shoulder and she whirled, red-rimmed darkness enveloping her. She didn't even feel the hard crush of asphalt against her face as she collapsed into unconsciousness.

13

Mack Bolan pulled around the corner in the jeep, and the smell of burning fuel met his nostrils, filling the soldier with a sudden jolt of dread. Lem Sengor tensed in the shotgun seat, and he glanced nervously at the driver.

"Trouble," they said at the same time.

Bolan stopped the jeep and got out, his rifle already in his hand. Sengor's Walther was locked in a secure, two-handed grasp, arms almost straight, but pointed at the ground. Zeki wanted to take part, but for the sake of not making the other Jandarma soldiers suspicious, neither Sengor nor Bolan had requested a sidearm for the youth. Bolan paused and handed the Jericho to the young Turk. "Stay with the jeep," he ordered.

Sengor translated, but Zeki was already nodding, understanding that the two older warriors, if they needed him, would want him covering their backs, not up front and in the middle of the conflict.

Zeki thumbed back the hammer on the big pistol and braced his forearms on the seat's headrest. Bolan noted with appreciation that Zeki's trigger finger was resting on the frame of the gun, not on its trigger. Then he and Sengor jogged forward, splitting to opposite sides of the street.

Divided, it would take their opponents longer to decide who to target first, giving both Bolan and Sengor more latitude in responding.

"Stone!" a voice called out from inside a building. Bolan paused and motioned for Sengor to wait.

"Ro?" Zeki shouted at the sound of his sister's voice.

"Talk to them," Bolan said. "I'll scout the wreckage."

Sengor looked at the column of smoke trailing from around the corner, then nodded, joining the boy as he reunited with his family.

Bolan left the scene behind him to check on Abood. She'd have told Ro to give him a message, but the sight of wreckage so close would bring the Executioner more up to date.

He reached the corner and poked out his head to look at the scene. A jeep was crumpled, smashed against a solid chunk of masonry. It was the only vehicle present, though. No bodies were strewed about the area, but gleaming on the asphalt, Bolan saw the brass shell casings from a rifle. He counted five. It was a short burst, more than enough to tear a person in two, since it was 7.62 mm NATO ammo. At short range, Bolan had seen and had torn targets to pieces with a quick squeeze of the trigger. He stalked forward, scanning the scene.

The jeep smoldered, its engine cracked and oil burning off hot engine parts. He circled the slab of stone and saw skid marks in the road, rubber laid down as if brakes had been applied to avoid a sudden crash. From the angle they were at, Bolan knew full well the vehicle had escaped a tragic collision. He looked at the wrecked jeep, and figured that Abood might have lured the hunter into a trap by whipping around the corner fast enough, using her own jeep to block the road. This would have forced a collision on the attacker's part.

But there had only been one hunter, Bolan realized. Looking at where the shell casings landed, the gunman had bailed out back at the corner. Since no bodies lay about, he was alone.

And he'd taken Abood's jeep, and her with it.

The coppery scent of blood cut through the smell of burned oil, and Bolan investigated it. It was still wet and fresh, a splash across the rock, a few droplets splattered on the asphalt. His jaw set grimly as he realized that Abood had been hit again. He was sure she was wounded. If she had been dead, she wouldn't have been taken along with the jeep. If she'd been victorious, she wouldn't have driven off with the gunman. How badly she was wounded was still a mystery at this point, but she was the captive of an unknown enemy.

Bolan heard Sengor come around the corner.

"What happened?" the man asked.

"Abood was taken. Only one man, with a rifle. And good reflexes. He avoided a crash by bailing out of his jeep," Bolan explained. "The kids?"

"They're fine. The little ones are bickering right now, but Aydin has them under control," Sengor replied. "It felt a little good putting their family back together."

"I hope they're not the last family reunited today," Bolan said. He glanced down the street at the trio. He looked back to Sengor, his mind on the task at hand. "He was by himself. Would Makal have been hunting around on his own?"

"He told us to split up, and sent me out by myself. But Makal would be packing a CZ-75, not an AK," Sengor replied.

Bolan raised an eyebrow.

"I saw the brass. They were thirties, not twenty-twos," Sengor explained.

"Good eyes."

The Turk nodded. "It was probably Boz Arcuri."

"That's who I narrowed it down to as well," Bolan mused. "He'd want both of us if Trug told him that we were responsible for his cousin."

"And she'd be live bait?" Sengor asked.

"Unfortunately," Bolan said. He pointed to the blood spatter. "He clipped her with a burst. Looks like only one bullet connected, but depending on where it hit, she'll be in a lot of trouble."

"I'm pretty good with first aid," Sengor answered.

"So am I. We just need to find her first."

"And that'll take time," Sengor murmured, realization dampening his words.

"Time that we can't afford if Makal is making a beeline to the warehouse," Bolan noted.

"He's more interested in looking for you. We weren't going to make our hit to recover the supplies until later tonight."

"They are moving them out tonight?"

"Tomorrow morning, before dawn. It was supposed to go out by truck. But now with the roads wrecked..." Sengor shook his head.

"They'll find another way," Bolan stated. "Which will mess with their timetable."

"Which means moving out early," Sengor replied. "How do you want to work this?"

Bolan looked at the splatter of blood. "Tell Aydin to take his brother and sister somewhere safe, then come back here and help me organize a game plan."

"You're going to hit everyone we know is guilty," Sengor replied.

"A familiar plan?"

"Makal does it all the time. Shake the cages, ruffle the feathers and see where everything flies," Sengor returned.

"It's a classic," Bolan replied. "You willing to get messy?"

"Absolutely," Sengor answered.

"Let Aydin have the jeep," Bolan told Sengor. "We'll find other transportation."

ABOOD'S SENSES RETURNED to her slowly. The first thing she noticed was that she was moving and then she heard the rum-

Get FREE BOOKS and a FREE GIFT when you play the...

LAS VEGAS
GAME

Just scratch off the gold box with a coin. Then check below to see the gifts you get!

YES! I have scratched off the gold box. Please send me my 2 FREE BOOKS and gift for which I qualify. I understand that I am under no obligation to purchase any books as explained on the back of this card.

366 ADL EEXG

166 ADL EEW4
(GE-LV-06)

FIRST NAME | LAST NAME

ADDRESS

APT.# | CITY

STATE/PROV. | ZIP/POSTAL CODE

7	7	7	Worth TWO FREE BOOKS plus a BONUS Mystery Gift!
🍒	🍒	🍒	Worth TWO FREE BOOKS!
🔔	🔔	♣	TRY AGAIN!

Offer limited to one per household and not valid to current Gold Eagle® subscribers. All orders subject to approval. Please allow 4 to 6 weeks for delivery.

ble of a jeep engine. A breeze against her cheek tossed her long black hair. She opened her eyes with an effort. They felt like they'd been gummed together.

She focused on the face of the driver, who glared at her, but continued driving. The man looked familiar, but she couldn't think of a name. She tried to move, but liquid fire exploded in her shoulder, in the muscle between her neck and collarbone. She also found that her wrists were bound tightly behind her. She turned her head, and despite the additional ache it inspired in her gunshot wound, she was able to rest her chin against a bandage taped to her shoulder. Her vest was gone, and she spotted the butt of her Beretta, poking out of the driver's waistband.

She tried to speak with him in Turkish. "Listen. I'm just a journalist—"

"You led them to my cousin," the driver answered in English.

"Boz Arcuri?"

"Good. You know the man who will kill you."

"I didn't want Recep to get hurt," she said. "I was trying to get him back—"

"So you and the American started a gunfight after he'd been tortured. It doesn't matter whose bullets killed him," Arcuri snapped.

Arcuri steered through the streets. Pedestrians in the road were too focused on searching for loved ones, or looking for help to notice a bound woman with a fresh gunshot wound.

As much as Abood would have appreciated help to escape Arcuri's death threat, she was glad for the bubble of indifference. If anyone tried to help out, Arcuri would have no qualms about murdering them.

No one could see that she was tied up as they drove past. The only good part of their presence was to slow the progress of the jeep.

It would give Stone a chance to catch up.

If Stone knew that she'd been taken, if he'd even survived Zeki's rescue.

The man proved to be a remarkable warrior, but there were limits even to his abilities. If she was going to get out of this, she'd have to rely on herself. Stone might sidetrack to help her, but that would only make it harder to get to the warehouse. It would give Arcuri's accomplices a chance to move the medical supplies.

"Listen—" Abood pleaded.

"To what?" Arcuri interrupted. "Lies? Pleas?"

"The medical supplies are needed. Look all around," Abood said.

Arcuri snickered. "Oh yes, appeal to my better nature."

"How about Recep? He was trying to help me recov—" Abood's head bounced backward from the force of the blow. Her shoulder burned in agony as she nearly fell out of the seat of the jeep. Arcuri's hand dug into her wound as he hauled her back upright.

Abood tasted blood in her mouth again. Three times in one day. She was starting to get sick of it. She spit it out, watching the mess splatter across her thighs.

"You talk about my cousin again, and I'll kill you. Got that?" Arcuri asked.

Abood kept her mouth shut, except to squirt out another blob of blood.

"Good," Arcuri muttered. "Now, we set you up as bait for the American and for Makal."

Abood's stomach tightened.

Makal. He'd be glad to silence her as a witness. If Arcuri had his way, Stone would walk right into a three-way firefight.

Something told Abood that this wouldn't be the first time he'd been in that situation.

The captive woman watched the sun crawl across the sky. It was getting to be late afternoon.

Time was running out.

BLOOD POURED OUT of the thug's mouth, and Makal felt a bit of satisfaction that he still had his touch. He angled the muzzle of the Walther between the Turk's lips and thumbed back the hammer. In the silence of the alley, the click of the draw focused the thug's attention.

"So what's the new plan?" Makal asked.

The thug, from the pipelike naked barrel jammed between his teeth, knew full well that the weapon wasn't Makal's legendary CZ-75. This was just another Walther—a throwaway gun. He could pull the trigger and end his life right there, and the death wouldn't be traced to the Jandarma captain.

With the aftermath of the earthquake, nobody would notice another corpse, even if the back of its head was blown off on the nose of a 9 mm bullet.

"The warehouse?" he murmured around the barrel.

"Yeah," Makal answered, easing the muzzle back to allow his victim to speak clearly. "They were going to drive up through Bardakci, but now with the roads all torn up, what's the new exit strategy?"

"They're skipping Bardakci. The boats are coming in from up there, at dawn tomorrow, and they'll just cut across to Adilcevaz," the man responded.

Makal frowned. "Any other news?"

"Just that Arcuri's gunning for the bastards who took out his cousin."

Makal leaned in closer. "And who's that?"

"The reporter. Catherine Abood. And the American man."

Makal nodded. "It will be a hell of a fight."

"He also mentioned your name," the Kongra-Gel snitch replied.

"Mine?"

"He has it in his head that you're part of this whole mess."

"And you believe him?" Makal asked.

"When Boz is on the rampage, we just let him go. Whatever happens, we stay out of his way. It's healthier like that."

Makal took a deep breath. "And you left that part until the end?"

The snitch nodded. "I'm sorry."

Makal shrugged. "So am I."

The snitch's brains exploded out of a funnel-like cavern in the back of his skull. Makal wiped the muzzle of his pistol on the thug's shirt, then turned and left the alley.

Another trembler rolled across the city, and bricks crashed in the alley behind Makal. He looked back and saw that his victim was half buried by the collapse of a damaged wall. He smirked and stuffed his gun back under his jacket.

"We should have more earthquakes," he muttered. "Makes things a lot easier."

He headed toward the warehouse. He was going to have to get his cut and blow its cover before they moved it all.

Makal had his retirement to think about.

BAYDUR TOOK A SIP of strong coffee to get his head back in order. He'd been overseeing relief efforts across the city, but it was taking a long time for information to get back and forth. The traditional landline phone grid was knocked out, with only a few calls able to make it through, and those that did were drowning in static. Those few who had cell phone technology were also in a bind. Several towers had been downed, and were now useless for relaying messages wirelessly. There were dead zones of communication throughout the city, and the radio frequencies were jammed as the authorities struggled to keep in contact with one another.

The latest round of tremors had spooked the citizenry.

Baydur looked at the parking lot that had been turned into a refugee camp. Thousands milled about, eyes wide. When the latest trembler hit, screams erupted.

Baydur didn't want to have to resort to riot-control measures, but the way the crowd was on edge, he was afraid he'd have to.

"Major?" Sezer interrupted Baydur's ruminations.

"What is it?"

"We've got a call for you about the earthquake situation," he said.

That surprised Baydur. "The phones are working?"

"It's a satellite phone that the army lent us," Sezer explained. "The call is from the minister of defense, Gordi."

"Good news?" Baydur asked.

"He didn't tell me, sir," Sezer responded. The assistant handed over the large green phone. It felt like it weighed fifty pounds, but since it was supposed to provide secure and reliable communication throughout the world, especially in the middle of a battlefield, Baydur didn't mind. He rested the brick of armored electronics on his shoulder.

"Baydur, reporting sir," he said.

"Omar, good to hear from you," Gordi responded. "I'm sorry about the situation I handed you."

"Cleaning up the Jandarma? Because I know the earthquake's not your fault, Cahil," Baydur replied.

"Well, I have good news on that front, Omar," Gordi responded. "The United States Navy is providing enhanced communications to the relief effort."

"They're already in the area?" Baydur asked.

"An aircraft carrier was stationed off Greece. At full speed, they were able to get in around noon today. They're sending out command and control aircraft, and they'll be arriving in about two hours," Gordi stated. "Now you'll be able to communicate with your troops better."

"That's great news!" Baydur answered. "But what's the

word on the earthquake situation? The whole city's still shaking like a belly dancer, and the refugees are getting skittish."

"I've been talking with my friend Bursa, from the Earthquake Observatory in Kandilli. We're going to be feeling regular aftershocks for the next three or four hours, and then they'll die off."

"How regular?" Baydur asked.

"Nothing definite, but according to their top seismologist, you won't be able to perceive them after about four hours. Or if you do, you'll just think it's a truck rolling past you," Gordi promised.

Baydur didn't hide the skepticism in his response. "Is that wishful thinking on their part?"

"I hope not. We'll just have to wait and see," Gordi replied. "Just tell your charges that nothing big is going to hit soon. The pressure that had built up is gone, and right now, the Earth's simply settling."

"That's what they told you?" Baydur inquired.

"In layman's terms. I'm not a scientist," Gordi responded. "If you want, I can put you in touch with Kandilli."

"No," Baydur said. "I probably wouldn't understand what they were talking about, either."

"Just trust them."

Baydur frowned. "Where I'm at, I'm having a hard time trusting anyone."

"Sir? Radio communications are opening up again. The airwaves aren't so jammed up now," Sezer stated. "We got a call in from Erdogan's camp."

"What happened?" Baydur asked, covering the mouthpiece so the conversation couldn't be heard.

"Erdogan was killed. Another was wounded. They held Sengor at gunpoint, but Sengor spun a tale about working with an Interpol inspector. Brandon Stone," Sezer explained. "Erdogan was supposedly in on the heist."

"I didn't know anything about this," Baydur said softly.

"Should I tell Erdogan's men to go after Sengor and Stone?"

"No. But see if you can raise Sengor on his cell phone. Let's see what he has to say about the situation," Baydur ordered. "What about Makal? Any word from him?"

"None," Sezer stated.

Baydur looked at the phone. This could possibly open a new can of worms that he didn't want to deal with, but he put it to his ear again. "Cahil?"

"What's wrong, Omar?" Gordi asked.

"I need you to do some checking. An Inspector Brandon Stone, with Interpol. See what you can pull up on him," Baydur answered. "We've got someone who's been sneaking around our back door. He just claimed that Erdogan was in on the theft of the medical supplies."

"Erdogan was with Makal's unit for a while, wasn't he?" Gordi asked.

"Yeah, but Sengor was the one who made that claim. And also claimed he's been working with this Interpol inspector."

"Smells fishy?"

Baydur's mouth turned bitter. "Smells like a rotting whale. Get me that info, okay?"

"I will," Gordi responded. "I know a few routes to get this data that there's no way Makal can interfere with. Take care of things on your end. I'll take care of them here."

Baydur hung up.

An Interpol inspector on the scene? he thought. What would he want with a midranked militia lieutenant tied to a crooked captain?

Something told Baydur that even if he found out the answers about Inspector Stone, he wouldn't be much closer to the truth.

Another trembler shook the ground, and the screams of the refugees drew him back to more pressing issues.

14

Stony Man Farm, Virginia

The night shift was well under way, but Barbara Price was manning the information center, a mug of strong coffee cupped in both hands. Without direct communications with Mack Bolan, the control center was only able to pick up on secondary information. So far, there had been one mysterious rescue reported, of a truckload of injured refugees. The details about the rescuer were sketchy, but they matched Bolan's description—tall, powerful, with piercing blue eyes.

"Way to go, Striker," Price whispered and she took another sip of coffee to keep awake.

"We're getting a hit on the search engines," Akira Tokaido announced. "Inspector Brandon Stone of Interpol."

"Inspector?" Price asked. "But Stone is Striker's military cover."

"Must have been a last-minute decision," Kurtzman spoke up. "Don't worry. We have protocols in place."

Price nodded. "I know we do. It just means that Mack's stumbled into something, and he hasn't had the time to properly build a cover."

"Next time he's in the middle of an earthquake and a civil war, we'll make sure he's better prepared," Kurtzman remarked.

"Damn it," Price snapped. "The Turkish state department is making the search."

"Based on an e-mail from the ministry of defense," Kurtzman noted, pointing to another subwindow. "Possibly the Jandarma is interested."

"Striker must be rattling some cages in Van," Tokaido added.

"We've dealt with sticky situations before. It's nothing new for us," Kurtzman said.

"The cover's in place," Akira announced. "As far as the Turkish government is concerned, Inspector Brandon Stone has been investigating, undercover, in the region for the past several months."

"We'll leak some more information if Striker ever gets back to us," Price responded.

"When he gets back to us," Kurtzman corrected her.

Price looked at the screen. "It's still feeling iffy to me. I hate it when Striker goes on an unsanctioned mission like this."

"Striker does what he does," Kurtzman replied. "It's not up to us to tie him down with rules or regulations."

Price took another sip of foul brew. "Just so we don't have to clean up the mess from this mission's aftershocks."

15

Tak Agar thought he was alone in the office at the back of his auto repair shop up until the moment a forearm dragged across his throat and yanked his head back until he thought his spine was going to snap. Cold fear shot through him, and he gurgled incoherently, but a hand clamped over his mouth.

"Makal told me that you speak English," Mack Bolan hissed in his ear. "Don't play dumb, and you get to live."

Agar trembled at the sound of the voice.

"I'm going to ask you questions. One finger for no. Two fingers for yes. Do you understand me?" Bolan asked him.

Agar, his neck bent, could only comply with the hand signals that Bolan had given him. He raised two fingers.

"Good. The next question is going to involve numbers. You can use both hands if you want. If you're lying, I begin to twist your head off your shoulders. Understand?"

Agar held up the yes sign again.

"How many men are here with you?"

Agar held up one hand, flashing four fingers.

Bolan gave a yank on Agar's chin that made the Turk's body convulse. He lost control of his bladder, and he quickly raised his other hand to indicate six men.

"You passed the test. Lies hurt. Truth hurts too, but it won't kill you."

Agar trembled in Bolan's iron grip. With the Executioner's knee jammed at the small of his back and his arms securing the Turk's head, even though his hands were free, he was helpless to do anything but answer Bolan's questions. The Kongra-Gel transportation coordinator had six of the roughest, meanest PKK enforcers in eastern Turkey working under him, and somehow Bolan had slipped past them and made his way into this office.

He also mentioned Makal. That filled Agar with a dread that weighed as heavily as Bolan's forearm against his trachea. The Jandarma captain was one of the few people in Van, aside from the Kongra-Gel high command, who knew that Agar was supposed to arrange transportation of the stolen medical supplies to a smaller port town.

"You're going to lend me a vehicle. You agree?"

Agar held up the yes sign. The further away this phantom of pain got, the better.

"You're going to send a message to Boz Arcuri as well."

"But—" Agar began but Bolan's hand clamped tight over his mouth, the forearm crushing harder against his throat. Tears flowed down Agar's cheeks. His pants were soaked with warm urine.

"If you make a sound again, I'll find another messenger."

Agar held up the yes sign again.

"Good."

Agar felt the pressure lessen on his throat.

"You'll find a way. You'll tell Arcuri that he has someone very important to me. She is to be released, unharmed. Then I'll give him his shot at the man who murdered Recep."

Agar raised two fingers.

"The phones are starting to work again. Burn up the lines with this message. Spread the word. I want Arcuri. And I want the woman unharmed."

Agar raised his fingers in the yes sign once more.

"Good. And tell the families of your goons that they'd better not follow in the dead men's footsteps."

Agar tried to turn his head.

"They're not dead yet," Bolan told him. "But it's coming in a moment."

The hand moved from Agar's mouth and pressed hard behind the corner of his jaw. Pressure built in the Turk's head and his consciousness swam dizzily around him.

A moment later, reality set in, crystal clear. He was in his office chair, wrists bound behind his back. Bolan pulled a pair of pistols and kicked open the office door. He turned and let Agar get a look. Except for those icy cold eyes, the American looked like a tall Turk.

Agar heard one of his men shout at the sudden racket.

Bolan turned away, both handguns raised, their muzzles blazing.

Gunfire split the air, the Executioner's body weaving and turning in a ballet of violence. If Agar hadn't known that every salvo of bullets had resulted in the death of one of his bodyguards, the Turk would have considered it a display of beauty. Instead, his stomach twisted and tightened.

After what seemed like an eternity, Bolan stopped shooting. He turned and walked back to the office, casually reloading each pistol as he walked behind the bound Kongra-Gel wheelman. Then Agar felt his wrists free.

"Make your phone calls," Bolan told him. "And pray we never meet again."

Agar watched Bolan turn and leave. He glanced down at the drawer, then at Bolan's back. He had a pistol with which he could...

"You'll never live to feel the grips of that gun," Bolan said, still walking. "Dial."

Agar reached for the phone.

One obeyed a god of vengeance when he gave you an order.

THE TOYOTA PICKUP TRUCK that Bolan had borrowed from Agar had a good suspension and four-wheel drive, making the trip through the earthquake-torn city much easier. Bolan had taken a few moments to rip the distributor caps out of the rest of Agar's fleet of vehicles, including the four large transports that he assumed were earmarked for hauling the Kongra-Gel's ill-gotten gains out of the city. Even though the Kongras wouldn't be able to take any roads out of the area, those trucks would have been enough to transport the stolen medical supplies to the docks where boats could pick them up.

Sengor's phone rang and the blond Jandarma cop answered it in the shotgun seat.

Bolan listened, following what he could as the Turk spoke in his native tongue.

"Sengor, here. What's up?"

"It's Baydur. I heard that Erdogan was killed, and that you're working with Interpol," came the answer from the other end.

"Yes," Sengor replied. "It's a little complicated, but—"

"Does he speak Turkish?" Baydur interrogated.

"It sounds like he knows a smattering," Sengor replied.

"I'll use English. Put him on the phone."

Sengor glanced at Bolan, and the Executioner took the cell.

"Stone," Bolan answered.

"Inspector, how nice to finally speak with you," Baydur's voice greeted over the phone.

"I wouldn't have been undercover if everyone knew who I was," Bolan responded. "Sorry for stepping on your toes, but we didn't know how far up the corruption in the Jandarma went."

"Which is odd," Baydur responded. "I was installed to deal with such corruption. How is it that you didn't touch base with me and my people? And why pick Sengor as your cat's paw?"

"Sengor was in a position to help me," Bolan responded. "You weren't."

"Interesting," Baydur responded. "And you felt it was necessary to kill Erdogan?"

"The lieutenant had a gun drawn and was going to kill Sengor and a teenaged boy. Neither Sengor nor I had any choice but to kill Erdogan before he murdered someone," Bolan said.

"Awfully bloodthirsty for an Interpol inspector," Baydur said.

Bolan was already growing tired of this line of questioning. "When I fired upon the other Jandarma men, it was either to wound, or suppressive fire not intended to hit any targets. Ask Erdogan's right-hand man."

"I did," Baydur stated. "It's unfortunate that you couldn't take Erdogan alive, though. So we could find out who else was allied with him."

"It was kill him, or let a boy be murdered. Besides, Sengor knows their network. He's been undercover with them for the past two years," Bolan answered.

"Two years. And how long have you been in country?" Baydur asked.

"I've been in and out of the country," Bolan stated. It was the truth. "Others usually have this watch. We kept on a rotation to insure that nobody was onto our operation."

"It sounds like an effective plan. This is the first I've even heard of all this," Baydur replied.

"Which is why we picked Sengor. He's a capable operative," Bolan responded. "Is there anything else you need to know? I've got business to attend to."

"Just a few more things, if you don't mind," Baydur said.

Bolan pulled the truck over. He was five blocks from his

destination, and he intended to walk the rest of the way. "Ask."

"Who do I contact in order to verify your credentials, Inspector Stone?" Baydur asked.

Bolan rattled off a name and a phone number. It was a cut-out number that would link through to Stony Man Farm from a "dead" phone number in Paris.

"Funny. You don't sound French," Baydur noted.

"I just work out of there. I'm Canadian," Bolan answered. He went with what he knew was his Interpol cover identity. He only hoped that any searches would alert the Farm to activate his Brandon Stone identity as such an agent, but he figured that Baydur wouldn't be speaking with him right now without nosing around a bit first. "On loan from the RCMP."

"A Mountie."

"And I always get my man," Bolan stated.

Baydur paused for a moment. "And your man wouldn't happen to be Yuli Makal, would it?"

"I can't give out any more details about the operation. Operational security," Bolan claimed.

"Understandable. Can I reach you through Lieutenant Sengor's cell phone?" Baydur asked.

Bolan gave him another number, one to a cell phone he already had active. "Since we seem to have better communication abilities, we'll use my unit. Just in case Sengor and I get separated."

"Thank you," Baydur replied.

Bolan had his phone already switched to vibrate, but Sengor's phone had no such function. "Don't call Sengor's phone. We're going to be nosing around, and I've shut his ringer off. You'll just drain his battery."

"I'll make a note of it," Baydur answered.

Bolan disconnected and handed the phone back to Sengor.

"Well, it's official. You're an Interpol intelligence asset," Bolan stated.

"Great. Does that mean I get a pay raise?" Sengor asked.

"We'll compensate you," Bolan replied.

Sengor blinked in surprise. "I was kidding."

"I'm not. Besides, now you won't have to explain your retirement fund. You can be on the straight and narrow," Bolan told him. "Well, as narrow as you can be fighting the Kurdish People's Party and their death squads."

Sengor nodded. "After the way you blew through Agar's men, it still seems a wide path."

"Desperate times. Desperate measures."

Sengor shrugged. "Works for me."

"Come on. We're running late for our next appointment."

Bolan got out of the truck and grabbed his HK. Unlike the last visit, there would be little need for stealth going in.

MAKAL PICKED UP THE PHONE. "What is it?"

"I got some news about Sengor," Sezer said.

"Don't leave me hanging."

"He's working with Interpol. And he just gunned down Erdogan."

Makal took a deep breath, his shoulders rising and falling as he struggled to control his anger. "How'd you find that out?"

"We've got communications backup, and just got a report from Erdogan's boys. Seems Sengor went to look in on their prisoners, and the next thing you know, Erdogan's getting ready to kill Sengor," Sezer replied.

"He never liked Lem. He thought he was a little too weak to be doing what we do best," Makal responded.

"Well, Lem wasn't as weak as we thought. He put three shots into Erdogan. The Interpol agent put a rifle round through his head."

"That leak's closed," Makal replied. "It's a loss, but it means more for us."

"I just don't want to join Erdogan."

"Then be careful," Makal answered.

"I just saw something else. Tak Agar got hit. Said you gave him up to some English-speaking guy. Big. Cold blue eyes. Death on two legs."

"The American," Makal commented.

"Agar's bodyguards are dead."

Makal almost choked. "All of them?"

Sezer sighed. "Six corpses. Multiple handgun wounds. And he's blaming you."

Makal's face twisted in rage. "Anything else from Agar?"

"Just that the American's looking for some woman that Boz Arcuri has," Sezer responded. "He's going to exchange her for the man who killed his cousin."

Makal's rage faded. "And you said that the American gave Agar my name?"

"Yeah," Sezer replied. "Sounds as if he's already carving you up and serving you as the whole feast."

Makal growled. "I'm not finished yet. If he wants my death, he's going to have to bring it to me."

"He's a few steps along that path already."

Makal killed the connection. It took him a few moments to calm down, but by the time he did, his mind had already sorted the situation out.

The mystery Interpol agent showing up, rescuing Sengor, and the American starting to feed Makal to the local Kongra-Gel jackals was tied together. The man who rescued Catherine Abood had to have lost her to Boz Arcuri, and when that happened, he turned to the only people who could feed him the information he needed to recover that nosy, meddling bitch. And since Makal was already on the American's list, from their previous encounter, he was turned into the pariah.

The man obviously wanted to recover the medical supplies, and not have to deal with the Jandarma captain and his coconspirators taking their cut. He was no Interpol inspector.

Makal had danced on multiple sides of the law enough to know the kind of man he was fighting against. The American was a mad-dog vigilante, some self-proclaimed champion who held no patience for any lawbreaking. He was as much an employee of the law as Makal himself was.

The American hunted men like Makal. He used illegal means, he killed his enemies, and he terrorized organizations, just like Makal had terrorized the PKK and later the Kongra-Gel. The American wasn't a law enforcer. He was a tool of justice. As much as Makal fought to cleanse the scum out of his city. But there was one difference.

Makal had bastards like Omar Baydur, and that cowardly minister of defense, Cahil Gordi, watching over him. Their predecessors had allowed Makal to run roughshod over whomever he wanted, just keeping the most gruesome business covered so that international pressure didn't hurt the Turkish government. But now, there was this talk of reform, and the puny bitches wanted Makal to treat these scumbags with kid gloves.

The American didn't seem to have such limitations.

Makal knew when they came face-to-face, only one man was going to walk away. And Makal wasn't ready to give up his retirement fund so easily.

LEM SENGOR CRAWLED into a roost overlooking the PKK safehouse. It was where the organization stored automatic weapons and explosives, stolen from the military. Bolan stood for a moment by the roost.

"You remember your speech?" Sengor asked.

Bolan nodded. "Thanks for translating it for me."

"You're good with languages," Sengor responded.

"Just make sure nobody sneaks up on me," Bolan said. He checked the taped rifle magazines. With a flip of the wrist, he could bring the empty rifle back into action. Aside from the forty shots in the weapon, Bolan had four extra magazines, as well as two Browning Hi-Power pistols that had been taken from the Jandarma thugs who had tried to kidnap Ro and Kandor Zeki. Since he'd fallen into a supply of Browning magazines, he'd resigned his HK to backup duty. Aydin Zeki had inherited the brawny Jericho and the remaining ammunition for it.

Bolan wished that he'd had the opportunity to find, or at least improvise, a sound suppressor for one of his pistols, but that would have to wait until after the hit on the Kongra-Gel armory. He still had to give Boz Arcuri the message that Catherine Abood was to be returned, without a hair harmed.

The Executioner walked up the middle of the street, and the two guards at the front of the Kongra-Gel armory—one of the few buildings relatively unaffected by the earthquake and its aftershocks—watched him in awe. Bolan stood in front of the sentries, holding the HK at port arms. One of the guards went for his rifle, but Bolan shook his head.

The guard stopped.

Bolan delivered his speech in Kurdish. "Boz Arcuri has a friend of mine. You two are going to live if you walk away and send a message to him. She is to be released, unharmed."

The sentries looked at each other, confused.

Bolan stepped forward. The second sentry reached for his gun, but the Executioner caught his wrist in an iron grasp. The first man glanced down to his rifle, but when he returned to watching Bolan, the muzzle of a Browning Hi-Power hovered an inch from his face.

"Walk away. Tell Boz Arcuri that he'll get a shot at the man who killed Recep Arcuri if he lets her go."

The guards looked at each other.

"Leave your guns behind."

The two sentries disarmed themselves and ran off. Bolan hung their rifles off a shoulder, then stuffed their handguns and spare magazines into a spare war bag that he had improvised from a book bag.

The door opened and a Kurd walked out. Bolan could make out that he was going to ask a question. It sounded as if he was going to ask the guards about coffee. Instead of getting an order for beverages, the newcomer got a face full of steel folding stock.

Head snapped back by the powerful blow, the Kurd dropped to the floor. Bolan dragged the stunned Kongra-Gel terrorist outside, then secured his wrists with a cable tie. The coffee man's handgun was added to Bolan's growing arsenal. He shouldered the war bag and walked into the PKK armory.

The time for sending messages was over. It was time to hit the Kongra-Gel thugs where they would hurt the most.

Gunmen raced out of doorways and from between crates.

Mack Bolan put mercy on hold and visited hell upon the savages.

LEM SENGOR WATCHED Bolan drag one guard from the Kongra-Gel stronghold.

"Why'd you leave this one alive?" Sengor asked.

"Extra insurance," Bolan said. He pulled a small black box from his pocket. "Fire in the hole," he shouted.

The armory disappeared in a thunderous flash. Bolan stood, already braced for the explosion, but Sengor was shaken to the core. The unconscious sentry woke from the noise and pressure wave washing over him.

Fluttering pieces of the building rained down like burning snowflakes. Bolan knelt and sliced the cable tie around the survivor's wrists, then slapped his cheek.

He repeated his speech in Kurdish for the newcomer, except for the line about dropping his guns, then hauled the Kurd to his feet and shoved him away.

The Kongra-Gel guard looked back at the crater where he'd been working only minutes before, and realized that he'd been granted a second chance by this grim wraith in black. The cold-eyed avenger standing before him wasn't joking around, so the guard raced away.

Sengor gave a low whistle. "Want to stick around Van for a while?"

"Trust me. This will stick in their memory for a long time."

"Do I get to take part in the next hit?" Sengor asked.

Bolan nodded and took off his war bag. He plucked a handgun from the pack and handed it over to Sengor. The Jandarma lieutenant looked at it and realized that it was a sound-suppressed Walther PPK.

"I got us some silenced handguns," Bolan explained. "The next visit is going to need some stealth and finesse."

"The bank?" Sengor asked.

Bolan nodded.

"Their wheels. Their guns. Now their money. Then the warehouse?"

"We'll get there soon enough," Bolan replied. "For now, we have business with Boz Arcuri and Makal."

"That was cold," Sengor spoke up.

"Giving his name to Agar?"

Sengor nodded. "You realize that Trug is going to put the heat on him and the strike force once the word filters back."

"You'll be fine with me," Bolan promised.

Sengor swallowed. "I wasn't exactly worried about myself—"

"Makal is poison," Bolan explained. "I just let the rest of the city learn that right now. You're covered with Baydur."

"Part of an Interpol investigation that doesn't exist," Sengor responded.

"It does now," Bolan replied. "I have friends who'll set it up."

"Fast as that?"

"Fast as that."

Sengor ran his fingers through his frosted hair. "Trug is still going to want a piece of me."

"That's why you're going to help me take him down."

"You're going after Trug too?"

"He wanted the medical supplies, and he's clearing them out of the city. He's the one stealing life from the refugees in this area," Bolan stated. "Just because he's the biggest and most powerful of the cannibals running through the region doesn't mean he's immune."

"In case you forgot, Trug has a small army covering his back," Sengor said.

Bolan looked at the smoking crater, then back at Sengor. "It's smaller now."

Sengor couldn't help but grin at that response. Wherever the man was going, the half-Kurdish soldier decided he wanted to follow.

The Executioner's war bag bulged with extra ammunition and explosives, and a large .357 Magnum revolver rode on his hip. A double shoulder holster housed a pair of sound-suppressed Walther PPKs, and a Browning rested in a cross-draw holster on his belt. Empty pockets were now heavy with small bricks of plastic explosives and detonators, or spare magazines for all of his weapons.

Sengor and Bolan headed back to the pickup truck.

16

Kagan Trug's voice exploded over the phone, but Boz Arcuri didn't wince. Finally, the Kongra-Gel commander's rage subsided, his curses fading.

"It's bad enough that Makal is handing the American everything he needs to wreck our operations in Van, but now I'm getting the pressure to have you turn over your prisoner," Trug stated.

Arcuri shrugged at the statement. "Prisoner?"

"Don't be coy, Boz. I'm talking about that journalist. Catherine Abood."

Arcuri looked over to Abood. He'd taken her shirt off, and where she'd been shot, he'd poured gunpowder over the bloody opening. A touch of a match, and the injury was cauterized instantly. It wouldn't do for her to bleed to death, or come down with an infection. Not before he had his chance to use her as bait. "Oh, her."

Abood, though pale and haggard, lifted her head.

Arcuri put his hand over the receiver. "Your boyfriend is worried about you, bitch."

Abood's lips twitched, not out of fear. Cold hatred stabbed from her dark eyes, and Arcuri chuckled. Now she felt like he did. He'd heard that misery loves company, but this was the first time he'd truly understood what that meant. A diabolic glee bubbled inside of him, his lips forming into a smile for the first time since he'd learned that his cousin had been murdered.

"You're going to die," Abood said, her voice harsh and dry.

Arcuri shrugged. "We'll all die someday, honey. But I'll rest assured that you and your friend will be in hell long before I am."

"Don't count on it," Abood growled.

"Boz, damn it!" Trug snapped loud enough for Abood to hear.

"Your master calls, Boz," Abood snarled. "Best tend to him."

Arcuri's good humor disappeared, and he considered shooting her again. "Sorry. My prisoner got talkative."

"Boz, what the hell are you thinking?"

"I'm thinking about killing two birds with one shot," Arcuri answered. "Makal and this Brandon Stone."

"In the meantime, our brothers are either slaughtered, or sent back to me with their tails between their legs, asking for her," Trug told him.

Arcuri frowned. "It's nothing we can't recover from."

"The transportation we need to move the warehouse supplies has been disabled. Jandarma forces are all over the garage!" Trug exclaimed. "And we just lost our armory."

"Guns and wheels can be replaced."

"And the men who died?" Trug asked.

"We are all called to make sacrifices for Kurdish freedom," Arcuri answered.

"You're about to become a sacrifice," Abood and Trug said in unison. Arcuri jerked, startled by the stereophonic response. The words seemed to carry an even greater weight, sounding like a prophecy spoken by a multivoiced god.

"You'll fold for this foreign bastard?" Arcuri asked.

"I'll kill you just to save my organization," Trug promised. "Give her up."

Arcuri nodded. "So, that's how it goes? Trading a true believer and warrior for the cause—"

"Warrior?" Abood snapped. "Warriors don't run and hide after leaving a bomb to blow up their enemies. Warriors aren't cowardly scum who kidnap women to use as—"

Arcuri stood up and crashed his fist into Abood's chin. She flopped off the chair and hit the floor, seeing stars from the impact. She tried to open her mouth, again full of blood, for the fourth time that day. But her jaw hurt too much to move. She couldn't even summon the strength to spit, rolling her head to let her blood and saliva drool out the corner of her mouth.

Arcuri had broken her jaw with a single punch, and her tongue ached, slashed by the chopping impact of her teeth.

"Going to say anything else, you lying whore?" Arcuri asked.

"Boz!" Trug demanded over the phone.

"Yes?" Arcuri answered, nonchalant.

"What did you do?" Trug asked.

"I think I broke the bitch's jaw. Don't worry, she's still alive," Arcuri promised. He prodded his toe into her side and chuckled.

Abood coughed and gagged, blowing the gory soup out of her mouth. She blinked and tried to roll on her shoulder, but the way her head had landed on the floor, she rolled onto the shoulder that had suffered the gunshot wound. Freshly scorched flesh wailed in agony at the weight applied and she slumped onto her back again, gasping for breath and spewing out choking bile. Tears burned down her cheeks from the pain, and the effort to sit up put enormous pressure on her broken jaw.

Arcuri helped her out, grabbing a fistful of her long black hair and yanking her upright.

Abood vomited right into her own lap, blood and bile ejecting out in a flood.

Arcuri stepped back and let her make a mess of herself. "You're going to have to stay like that."

"Damn it, Boz!" Trug snapped. "If she dies…"

"If she dies, she dies," Arcuri responded. "Your cousin wasn't murdered. Mine was. Stone. Makal. Every one of them. They'll pay. They'll burn. And when this jezebel dies, she'll be glad for the hell she goes to."

Arcuri knelt in front of Abood. "Isn't that right?"

Catherine Abood's jaw was frozen with pain, but she managed to spare enough strength to spit a chunky, red blob at Arcuri's face.

The Kurdish terrorist hung up on Trug and exploded into laughter again.

"Misery does indeed love company," Arcuri told her. He wiped the smear off his face and ran his fingers through her hair. She struggled to get away, but Arcuri squeezed her chin, made all the more agonizing for her broken jaw.

Arcuri laughed again and wiped his blood-and-vomit smeared hand on her pants.

"Thanks for making my day," Arcuri told her.

Laugh it up, asshole, she thought. Because this is the last day you'll be alive.

THE KURDISH GUARD STEPPED out back, his rifle in one hand leaving the other hand free to light his cigarette. He looked up to see the Executioner holding a silenced Walther PPK. Before the sentry could shoot, Bolan pulled his trigger. A slug smashed through the gunman's lips and tore out the back of his head. The corpse slumped against the wall, the cigarette still dangling from the corner of his mouth.

Bolan took the butt and flicked it down the alley. "Those things are hazardous to your health."

He opened the door and Lem Sengor swung through into the back room. Two more guards, playing cards, jerked upright at the sudden entry of the intruder. Sengor lifted his handgun and paused for a heartbeat.

Bolan stepped in and punched another shot into one of the guards. Sengor steeled himself and fired twice into the remaining guard before the Kurd even had a chance to react.

"No messenger?" Sengor asked.

Bolan shook his head. He reloaded his sound-suppressed pistol and put it back in its holster. He unslung the HK G-3. Holding the rifle with one hand, he jerked the corpse he'd shot in the head to its feet, wiped a trickle of blood off its face and dragged it to the metal door leading to the PKK vault.

Bolan nodded to Sengor, who rapped on the door, shouting for someone to open up. Bolan pushed the dead man's face close to the slot as it opened.

"What's going on?" the man on the other side asked.

"I gotta take a piss!" Sengor replied. "Let me in."

"Damn it! Just use the alley," the guy on the other side answered.

"Damn you. I'm tired of being treated like an animal," Sengor returned.

"If I get reprimanded—"

"You can explain the rust on the door from my piss. Now open up!" Sengor told him.

The door unlocked. It creaked open a tiny bit, and Bolan hurled the corpse aside. He rammed his foot into the door and slammed it open hard. The man who answered was hit by the metal door and knocked aside.

Another guard jerked toward the doorway in reaction, but Bolan was already halfway through, his G-3 ripping off a short burst that tore the Kurd open from crotch to throat. The other sentry tried to get out from behind the door, but the Executioner leveled the G-3, single-handed like a pistol, and hammered out another blast of slugs that pulped the guy's face and skull.

"I guess they know we're here now," Sengor stated.

Bolan moved, silent, weapon tracking. He was blitzing in full effect now, and any conversation was just another distraction. He cut through a doorway and spotted Kurdish Turks frantically trying to sweep money into bags in response to the sudden raid. One of them reached for a handgun to ward off the Executioner, but a salvo of 7.62 mm hornets pulverized a gaping crater in the center of his chest.

The others spoke wildly, probably offering Bolan bribes, but he held down the trigger and fanned the room. Turkish money notes flew in a blizzard of colors, some sprayed with brilliant, fresh red as the money handlers jerked in death dances. When the G-3 clicked empty, Bolan flipped the taped magazines and chambered a fresh round.

There was one man left, clutching his shoulder where it had been punctured by a rifle slug. His dark eyes stared in wild terror at the grim, implacable gunman looming over him.

Bolan repeated his Kurdish speech, pressing the hot muzzle against the Kurd's cheek. Skin smoked as it fried on sizzling metal. "Captain Makal sends his regards."

Bolan nodded to Sengor, who grabbed two full bags of money. The Executioner leaned down and picked up the wounded man and hurled him through the doorway. Sengor had brought in a canister of gasoline with him, and left it behind when he evacuated with the wounded man, all part of Bolan's plan.

The Executioner tore off the cap and splashed flammable fuel across the remaining money and corpses. He threw the container in the corner, pulled out a disposable lighter and fired it up.

The money room was an inferno within half a minute, but by then, the Executioner was already en route to his next war zone.

Word of the Kongra-Gel's worst nightmare spread almost as quickly as the fire in the money room.

Which was just as the Executioner wanted it.

CAPTAIN YULI MAKAL stepped into the street after shaking down another of his snitches. This one he left alive, but bleeding. His mood was better after popping the head of the first snitch, but not enough to show the next scumbag much mercy.

He was lucky that he looked both ways as he stepped out into the open. A jeep raced toward him, filled with men with guns. Makal hit the deck as a storm of autofire cut the air over his head, and he unleathered his CZ-75 in one smooth motion. Normally, rifles against a handgun would be no contest.

In this case it was. But Makal was under their line of fire. Most PKK veteran fighters were only good at holding down a trigger and spraying bullets, hoping to hit a target by God's will.

The Turkish captain, however, was a marksman, and an expert shot with his 9 mm pistol. While the Kongra-Gel hit men wasted the contents of their assault rifles' magazines, Makal's first two shots were centered on the driver as the jeep passed by.

Twin parabellum manglers chopped under the driver's arm and he jerked violently. The dual impacts forced the man at the wheel to lurch sideways. He steered wildly off course, and the front of the vehicle crumpled as it wrapped around a lamppost. Heavy wrought iron crushed the jeep like a loaf of bread, and riflemen tumbled out of the sides of the vehicle, scattering like twigs in a wind storm. The driver didn't feel the crash, however. He was dead before they hit.

Makal got to one knee and swung his front sight at a Kongra-Gel gunman who scrambled to reach his rifle. The CZ-75 barked again, and the Kurd stopped in his fast crawl, as if he'd struck an invisible brick wall. Makal's bullet had taken him at the bridge of his nose, and one more Kurdish insurgent sprawled lifelessly in the street.

Makal got to his feet and walked toward the carnage he'd inflicted. One of the Kurdish outlaws screamed, holding his shattered, bloody leg. Bones stuck out through his thigh, and he wailed for help and mercy. Makal provided it to the wounded man, in the form of a trio of bullets into his head.

"Quiet. You're disturbing the peace," the Jandarma captain hissed.

There was one last rifleman from the jeep, and he curled against the side of the crushed vehicle. His guns had been flung far away from him, and he whimpered, in tears.

"I was just following orders!" the frightened thug cried.

Makal tilted his head as he raised the handgun.

"Please! No!" the would-be assassin howled, covering his face and head with his arms. "I give up! Don't kill me!"

Makal grabbed the Kurd's forearm and pulled him to his knees and pressed the muzzle of the hot pistol against his victim's cheek. "Go back to Trug and tell him that anyone he sends against me is going to end up either lying in their own blood or sitting in their own piss, just like you."

"But it wasn't Trug. It was Agar," the Kurd said, frightened, but emphatic. "Please... I just want to live."

"Then phone it in to Trug that Agar is going against the wrong man," Makal warned. "He's not going to enjoy your failure."

The weeping man coughed and sputtered, resting his cheek against Makal's thigh. "I am in your debt—"

The Jandarma captain brushed the Kurd away. "Don't push your luck."

Makal turned and went back to his car.

Trug hadn't found enough time in his busy schedule to let Agar know that Makal wasn't behind the screw job that hit him. If that was the case, then Kagan Trug had to be cutting his losses.

There was one small problem with that. The Jandarma captain didn't consider himself a loss. That was okay with Makal, though. By declaring war, Kagan Trug had put himself on the little dinner party list Makal was building. And the first item, the only item, on the menu was going to be a face full of blazing hot lead.

IT TOOK AWHILE, but Baydur finally got Jandarma command to move in a small squadron of Turkish military Black Hawk multirole helicopters. He also managed to get some older Cougars. They were tired workhorses, but they still could do the job as well as the Black Hawks.

Baydur was reluctant to use any of the Black Hawks or Cougars for his personal transportation, but when Gordi had arranged for an OH-58B Kiowa, Baydur felt relieved. The smaller helicopter couldn't transport the wounded or supplies with the same versatility as the multipurpose Black Hawks and Cougars. The Kiowa was an observation and scout craft, and was also used as a VIP transport in civilian operations. Baydur and Sezer clambered on board as soon as they received the call about an inferno blazing at a suspected Kongra-Gel hideout.

It gnawed at Baydur's gut that there was still a war going on amid the relief efforts. He knew that, somehow, Sengor and Inspector Stone were involved in this sudden rash of combat.

Sezer's phone rang, and he plucked it out of his pocket, plugged in the hands-free cable to connect to his helmet and then took himself out of the circuit. The driver began speaking quickly and softly.

"What's going on?" Baydur asked.

Sezer held up his hand. The thump of the rotors overhead made it impossible to hear what Sezer was talking about, and the way his head had turned, Baydur couldn't even read his lips. Sezer's head jerked upright, and he glanced over to

Baydur. He clicked back into the main communications circuit. "It's Makal. He wants to talk to you."

"You're alive, Captain," Baydur spoke up.

"And lucky to be alive," Makal's voice answered. "Agar just sent a crew to take me out. Says I'm responsible for knocking over his garage."

"We heard about the hit, but we don't have anything on who was behind it," Baydur replied. "He's blaming you?"

"Someone dropped a bug in Agar's ear that I gave up his operation," Makal stated. "I took out three of the killers who came after me, but it's not going to be an easy day if the Kongras are looking to kill a bunch of Jandarma soldiers during this whole mess."

"Think it's related to the stolen medical supplies?" Baydur asked.

Makal was silent for a moment, then he recovered his voice. "Probably. They want us to get defensive. When that happens, they can move whatever weight they want out from under our noses."

Baydur sighed. "Did you ever hear anything about Sengor working with an Interpol inspector?"

"What?" Makal asked. Rage washed out in that response. "No. Nobody told me anything."

Sezer's shoulders relaxed for a moment, and Baydur wondered at that sudden moment of relief.

"Well, you're in on it now. Interpol's been investigating the Kongras and their possible moles inside the Jandarma. If there's any dirt inside your strike force, you'd better let me in on it right now," Baydur said.

"Just the usual confidential informant crap. Cutting deals, looking the other way so that we can work our way up to bigger fish," Makal responded. "Why?"

"I'm thinking that we're going to have a lot of dirty secrets shaken out of our trees today. The earthquake seems to have loosened up the whole world, and I'm not liking what I'm seeing," Baydur told him. "If you've got something rotten you're hiding, make sure it's buried deep and it doesn't come back to haunt the Jandarma."

"Are you accusing me of—"

"Give me a break!" Baydur snapped. "I know how you operate. I hear the stories from the street too. If you think you can convince me that you're innocent, you must think I really am a simpleton."

"That goes without saying, you paper-shuffling ass," Makal retorted. "What I do gets results. You'd give these murdering bastards milk and cookies and hope that they'd go away."

"So that's how it is?" Baydur asked.

"Yeah. And by tonight, Kagan Trug and his whole operation is going to come crashing down. If you want to be a part of it, sign on with me. Otherwise, keep out of my way. You're either with me, or you're against me."

"Do what you do," Baydur ordered. "Just know that if you fall down, I'm not picking you back up and wiping the blood off your face."

"If I fall down, there's not going to be anything at all to pick up."

Baydur smiled. "That's the best news I've heard all day."

17

Lem Sengor didn't notice the arrival of the newcomers until it was almost too late, but that didn't really matter. He was hauled off his feet and thrown to the ground an instant before the world exploded into a symphony of autofire that ripped the air to staccato chunks. Brass tumbled in a golden rain out of Bolan's G-3 as the Executioner swung into action, the empty casings bouncing off Sengor's head and face.

The Jandarma officer rolled out of the way and brought his rifle to bear, squeezing off bursts as fast as he could at the racing figures charging at them. Before he could fully analyze what was going on, the ground was littered with the corpses of riflemen—three of them—and others had scrambled for the cover of rubble and crushed vehicles. Finally, the confusion left Sengor's mind as he identified the attackers.

"Kongra-Gel," Sengor stated.

Bolan had crouched behind the frame of a dented Peugeot and fed his G-3 a spare magazine. "That was my bet too. They're not wearing uniforms, and they're not packing HK rifles."

Sengor shouldered his G-3 and triggered a short burst that caught one of the half-concealed Kurdish gunmen at head level. The salvo of NATO slugs decimated the terrorist's skull, spraying gooey blood and brains in an ugly fountain of death.

"Keep their heads down," Bolan told Sengor. He reached

into his war bag and pulled out a pair of grenades. Sengor triggered more bursts, but his first kill was just a fluke. The other Kongra-Gel assassins had knuckled down tighter, trying to avoid suffering the same decapitation as their friend. The recoil of the G-3 on full-auto jolted the Jandarma lieutenant's shoulder, but he kept up the heat. The pounding of the wire stock hurt a hell of a lot less than the pounding of an enemy bullet.

The G-3 locked empty and Sengor ducked back down. "I hope you've got something in mind."

Bolan looked both ways, then flipped Sengor a grenade. "We're clear. Toss 'em."

Sengor plucked out the cotter pin and lobbed his bomb into a high arc. Bolan whipped his in a sidearm toss before getting back behind cover. Their explosions came in one unified shock wave that shook the small alley. Screams and wails assaulted Sengor's senses as he looked around. No one was left in a mood to fight, but he still reloaded his G-3 before stepping into the open. The Executioner led the way and Sengor looked around. There wasn't the kind of char damage, or spatter that he would have expected from fragmentation grenades. What he did see were men, clutching their ears and screaming in pain. Some had blood leaking from their noses and mouths, but all had been downed instantly.

"Concussion grenades," Sengor noted.

"Hurts like hell, but they're going to live," Bolan said.

"Aren't they the bad guys?" Sengor asked. "I mean, we gunned down enough of them."

Bolan grabbed one of the least dazed and hauled the Kurd to his feet. He glared into the man's eyes for a long moment, then let him go, throwing him aside like a rag doll.

Thoroughly cowed, the Kongra-Gel hit man crawled backward, away from the pair.

"I've established my dominance over the situation," Bolan

stated. "If they still have the heart to come after me, I'll burn them down."

"'For to win one hundred victories in one hundred battles is not the acme of skill. To subdue the enemy without fighting is the acme of skill,'" Sengor recalled. "Sun Tzu. *The Art of War.*"

Bolan nodded, and the Jandarma man smiled, getting the point. "Tell them that if they feel like burning off some hostility, help with the relief effort. Otherwise, get out of the city."

Sengor translated for the Executioner, repeating himself as the stunned gunmen couldn't believe their ringing ears. They all looked at the tall wraith in black, standing like a pillar of darkness.

"Go now!" Bolan snapped in a respectable Kurdish.

The Kongra-Gel gunners broke and ran for their lives.

"No more messages to Arcuri?" Sengor asked.

"That was his message back," Bolan explained. "He's got hunters out across the city."

"You sure they were meant for us?"

Bolan glanced at the crew as they disappeared. "Yeah. They were willing to try to take the both of us out. So they either recognized you, or they recognized me."

"We need to stir up the nest, and I want them to know exactly who they're facing," Bolan said. "Come on. No rest for the wicked, and those who hunt them." Bolan turned and led Sengor back to their jeep.

CATHERINE ABOOD LIFTED her head. It took all of her strength, and as soon as her wobbly head settled on her neck, she saw Boz Arcuri setting up one more brick of plastic explosives. She tried to open her mouth, but the duct tape slapped over her lips kept her silent. The jolt of searing lightning that shot through her broken jaw as she endeavored to speak kept her from trying again.

Breathing heavily through her nose, Abood looked as Arcuri walked back to her.

"Having trouble?" Arcuri asked.

Abood could only answer with cold hatred smoldering in her dark eyes.

"Let me help."

The duct tape was pulled away in one flash of agony. Her lips were raw and stung from where the adhesive yanked the top layer of skin off. She gagged and sputtered.

"Word of advice," Arcuri told her. "I'm not here to help you."

"Noticed," Abood muttered, her jaw throbbing in pain.

"Glad we understand each other," Arcuri replied. "So, ready to be at ground zero?"

Abood looked around again. Tiny LEDs burned like the eyes of rats around the warehouse floor. "Where—"

"You passed out, so I decided to bring you to where everyone wants to be," Arcuri answered. He tapped her cheek gently.

Abood's neck ached and her head slumped. As she squinted, she felt something crack on her forehead, and blood trickled down into her eye. She winced and recoiled and that only increased the surge of pain that stampeded through her skull.

Arcuri slapped her forehead injury with another length of duct tape, then splashed a cup of water in her eyes. She blinked the water away and recovered her senses in a moment.

"Sorry. The bandage on your forehead finally gave way. The duct tape will help some. Though, I won't say too much for how your face will look if someone does manage to rescue you," Arcuri said. He slapped his own forehead. "What am I thinking? You're dead anyway."

"Too scared to face Stone?" Abood asked.

"I just want to give the maximum bang possible," Arcuri

replied. He showed her something that looked like an electronic dumbbell. "This is a dead-man switch. You know what those are, right?"

Abood nodded. It was all her brain could take. Even moving her head slightly made the inside of her skull slosh around like the contents of a washing machine.

"If your friend shows up, or if Makal shows up, even if Trug and the whole of the Kongra-Gel show up, and they somehow get past me, I lose my grip on this trigger," Arcuri explained.

"Scorched earth," Abood said. She could get out one or two syllables before the pain became too much.

"Exactly. See, Kagan Trug is setting me up to be a sacrifice. Makal, he killed my cousin. Stone, he was part of that cross fire—"

"Wrong," Abood interrupted.

"No?" Arcuri asked. "Probably right. Trug just wanted me to go after him, to keep him out of his hair."

Abood's eyes narrowed. "And…the…supplies?"

"Must hurt to talk, huh?"

Abood didn't dignify the Kurd with an answer, except for another glare of hard rage. If she could have gritted her teeth without making her eyes explode out of their sockets, she'd have bared her bloody teeth for him.

Arcuri simply chuckled. "The medical supplies? Meant for whom? More money in the pockets of bastards who want me dead? Slugs willing to kneel under a corrupt government? Tell me why I should care about anyone anymore."

Abood took a deep breath. "Recep."

Arcuri grabbed her, squeezing her cheeks with his thumb and forefinger. The pain turned everything behind her eyes into a brilliant orange haze of liquid fire. "He was the only good thing in this rotten hellhole. Now he's dead, and with his death, I've learned the truth about the world. Life is a steaming pile of dung."

Abood thought she was going to pass out when he finally released her. Bile churned, but she didn't have enough left in her for it to do anything other than to burn acridly at the back of her throat. If she was going to die, she couldn't imagine any hell being worse than this one.

"Can you name anything good and just in this world?"

Abood glared. She was almost ready to pass out. Too much pain from aggravated broken bones and blood loss and cauterized gunshot wounds. To pass out would be to collapse into a state of numb bliss. But she couldn't let Arcuri go unanswered. "Stone."

The Kurdish madman nodded. "That would make sense. Someone you care about. Well, when I blow up the both of you, there won't be any goodness left in the world, will there?"

Abood tensed. "You're insane."

"Why is it that everyone considers those who are sane and in control mad?" Arcuri asked. "The world is clear for the first time in my life. Nobody cares. We're all killing and eating each other, psychotic little parasites. This morning, I was awakened by the Earth herself, trying to shake the fleas from her back. Many were crushed, though not quite enough. But don't worry. I'll take care of a few more ticks nibbling on her."

"Fucking nuts," Abood continued.

Arcuri cupped the tip of her chin with his finger, and she tilted her head up to relieve the sudden, agonizing pressure. His fetid mouth pressed to hers, tongue invading her mouth like some burrowing slug. Her jaw flared with agony, nerves misfiring as her broken mandible flexed.

The darkness Abood wanted moments ago fell upon her, granting her the sweet sleep of oblivion.

MAKAL DIALED HIS CELL PHONE as he drove.

"Yuli?" Sengor's voice asked on the other end.

"Yeah, what's up?" Makal returned. "I hear something about you and some Interpol spook."

"Just covering my ass," Sengor replied. "The truth is a lot more complicated,"

"Tell me about it," Makal ordered. Sengor remained silent for a long time. Then he heard the phone changing hands.

"Makal. It's me." The voice was deeper, stronger. It resonated through the phone.

"Stone?"

"Speaking," Bolan answered.

"Why are you leaning on me?"

"I've got a laundry list, but I'll stick with first impressions," Bolan told him.

Makal chuckled. "You mean that nosy reporter?"

"It wouldn't matter who she was. I saw a gang of rapist thugs," Bolan explained. "The fact that you kill whoever Trug turns you onto, to stir up recruitment for him, that's icing on the cake."

"Do you really think you know how it works here?" Makal asked.

"It works the same way it does around the world. A savage dresses himself in patriotism, in 'doing the right thing' and uses that as his justification to commit atrocities. That's about my take on you, Makal."

"Well, Baydur just spoke with me. He told me to bury this mess, so how about we meet face-to-face?" Makal asked.

"Sure. Call in all the friends you need," Bolan offered. "Even five of you couldn't handle one reporter."

"Provoking me?" Makal asked. "Trying to get my head out of my game so that I get sloppy?"

"Doing what I can," Bolan admitted. "How about we meet at the warehouse? After all, Trug isn't going to have any manpower to take the drugs away."

Makal laughed. "Seems we're all heading there, doesn't it?"

"Well, I think I'll be in the area picking up a friend. My offer still stands. Bring everyone you want. I'll plant them," Bolan repeated.

"Is that so?" Makal asked. "I never picked you for someone who pisses testosterone."

"I know I piss someone off," Bolan chided. "I'll see you at the warehouse."

"Put Sengor back on," Makal snapped.

"Sure."

The phone changed hands again. "Yuli?"

"You're either with me, or you're against me. You know the rules," Makal threatened.

Makal heard a grunt on the other end.

Sengor answered. "Yeah. The rules. Skinning kids and raping helpless women. All to anger the likes of Boz Arcuri?"

"So you're against me?" Makal said.

Sengor's voice was strained and brittle. "I'm just sorry it took me so long to wake up."

"I should have known your muddy blood would stop feeding your brain one day, Lem," Makal said.

"It's all about the racism. You just can't see—"

"You can't see that the families of these jackals are as much fair game as they are," Makal told him. "They support these murdering idiots, and when we come down on them, these 'innocents' are still out there, breeding hate, giving their friends support, building—"

"So you cut up a fourteen-year-old boy?" Sengor asked. "What kind of insanity is that?"

Makal nodded. "Erdogan was right about you. You're soft."

"Not anymore," Sengor replied. "You're going down, Yuli."

"You and what army?" Makal asked.

"I just need one soldier," Sengor told him. "The guy you just spoke with."

Makal sneered. "You're going to get that holy? Your money was tied up in our operation against Trug too, you smug bastard!"

"I got back my investment," Sengor returned. "I got back my soul."

The phone clicked off.

Makal almost hurled it out of the jeep, but then he controlled himself.

He needed to call in some backup.

THE HELICOPTER SWUNG slowly over the street. Smoke poured from a grenade, dropped by Lem Sengor and his mystery Interpol inspector, and Major Baydur braced in the doorway.

Sezer sat beside him, pistol in hand, ready to leap to Baydur's defense. The Jandarma commander hopped off the landing rung the last couple of feet to the ground and approached the pair. Inspector Stone was a tall, imposing man with cold blue eyes. His face was covered in grime from the day's efforts, and his jaw had all but blackened with five-o'clock shadow. If it wasn't for those icy eyes, he would have fit in without a second glance with the Turk and Kurdish population in Van. As it was, he greeted Baydur in a very passable Turkish greeting.

"Please, English is fine," Baydur answered, doffing his headset. He glanced back to Sezer, coiled in his seat like a snake. He returned his attention to Sengor. "You spoke with Makal lately?"

"Yes," Sengor answered. "He's not too happy with us."

"Seems he doesn't like Sengor being undercover and reporting about Makal's torture activity," Bolan stated. "Torture. And stirring up the hornet's nest in order to keep his job security."

Baydur stepped closer. "And you gunning down members of his group was supposed to help that?"

"Right. Gunning down armed rapists in the process of violating a human being," Bolan returned. "I should have never gotten involved in saving a life."

Baydur glared for a moment, then broke into a smile. "Makal said that he was detaining a witness to the murder of Recep Arcuri."

"Makal also says that he's in the right when he skins teen-aged boys and girls related to Kurdish Party members," Sengor snapped. "So we're supposed to believe all of that?"

"I know. Makal's file is one I've flagged for investigation. I just haven't been able to find anything on him yet," Baydur replied. "I almost got you to help me out earlier today, remember?"

Sengor nodded. "You're trustworthy. But…"

Sezer came out of the helicopter and walked over to them. The craft's engines powered down, and there was less background racket. Baydur noticed that Sezer's pistol was still firmly grasped in his hand.

"Yes, there are potential leaks in the Jandarma," Baydur mentioned. "I've tried my best to vet all of my staff."

Sezer's hand trembled.

Baydur took a step back.

Sezer lifted his handgun, but Bolan took a quick step forward and twisted the weapon out of the man's grasp. Fingers snapped like twigs and Sezer howled in agony. With a jerk, the Executioner hauled Sezer to the ground, twisting his arm into a painful chicken-wing shape.

Baydur pulled his weapon and leveled it at Sezer. "You fucking little turd."

Sezer whimpered, the pressure on his arm almost enough to break it. Bolan's grasp was designed to induce a world of pain to any prisoner, yet not do permanent damage. Just an ounce more force, though, and the limb would be reduced to a useless lump of hanging muscle and bone.

"You won't need the gun," Bolan said, reverting to Turkish.

He leaned closer. The added pressure of Bolan's new leverage dropped a curtain of agony that choked off Sezer's whimpers and pleas for mercy. "You don't want me to rip out your arm, do you?"

"No," Sezer grated. He could barely get any other words out. Sweat soaked the Jandarma traitor's hair to his forehead, and his dusky skin reddened from pain.

"Makal needs some backup, people he trusts," Bolan prompted. "How many?"

Sezer sucked his lips between his teeth. A nudge tilted his shoulder enough that tendons cracked and popped, sounding like the firing of a submachine gun. "Ten."

Bolan glanced back to Sengor, who nodded.

The Executioner eased his pressure on Sezer's arm.

"You can take care of the rest," Bolan told Baydur.

"You're not going to ask for some backup yourself?" Baydur asked.

"It'd make things too complicated and give the enemy too many targets to shoot at," Bolan answered. "I want to limit the damage I'm doing to the Jandarma, and any honest men you can assemble are better put to work with the earthquake relief efforts."

"Besides," Sengor added. "Putting the call out to bring down the hammer on Makal—"

"Sezer wouldn't be the only leak," Bolan interjected. "Makal can count on ten guns to back his play, but he's probably got informants through the whole system."

"So, what can I do to help?" Baydur asked.

Bolan leaned in closer. "Get word to your contact in the defense ministry. We'll need to get the medical supplies out of the warehouse the moment we get control of it."

"I'll see what I can do," Baydur promised.

"We just need a cleanup," Bolan explained. "And the medical supplies distributed as fast as possible."

"We've got the helicopters coming in. A U.S. aircraft carrier is sending relief support too. They'll be here by midnight," Baydur said. "I assume that's good news to you."

"Good enough," Bolan replied. "Just make sure nobody misappropriates it. Too many—"

"I know," Baydur answered. He glared at Sezer, who was still in Sengor's custody. "Too many people died for it. These damned vultures want to make money while people are dying."

"He'll want to make a deal," Bolan noted. "It's your choice—you can clean out the rest of his brood, and let him walk…"

Baydur chuckled.

Bolan looked at him for a moment, then nodded.

"Live by the sword, die by the sword," Baydur said in Turkish. "Or, in your case, turncoat, lose your skin by the sword."

Sezer's lips quivered and he looked pitifully at Bolan and Sengor. He began pleading in Turkish, but the Executioner only pulled out a combat knife and handed it to Baydur.

The helicopter pilots helped hold down Sezer, while Bolan and Sengor headed for their confrontation with Makal and Arcuri.

It took five minutes of walking before they couldn't hear the screams for mercy anymore.

18

This was the building that it was all about, Gogin thought. The sun had crawled behind the roof, casting the building in darkness. The concrete canyons behind him were shrouded in early-evening shadow, making the city seem like a ghost town.

He shut down the jeep and pulled his G-3 off the seat beside him. Two more pickup trucks pulled up. No one had their headlights on, not wanting to spook anyone on the inside.

The warehouse was an unimpressive building, overlooking the briny lake. The smell of salt wafted off the water, overpowering the scent of blood so that Gogin didn't notice it until he saw the splotches at one of the side doors. It took a moment to notice the streaks leading up the walls of the warehouse, and then he saw the men hanging, feet swaying in the wind, hollowed bellies fluttering like the tails of jackets.

Gogin fought back nausea, though it was hard as he heard two of his fellow Jandarma enforcers lose the contents of their stomach.

"Quiet," he whispered. "Keep it under control."

"Sorry, sir," one of the men replied. He wiped bile from his lips. "It's just—"

"Yeah," Gogin answered. "It's bad. Whoever's inside is pretty damned dangerous. And insane. Lock and load and kill anything you see."

The assembled Jandarma crew nodded. The pickup trucks were going to be loaded up with the medical supplies that Makal had marked for their personal use. Once they grabbed the stuff and got it out of the area, then they'd call in more support and deny the Kongra-Gel its ill-gotten loot. And Makal's strike force would walk away with a good chunk of money.

Now, the madman who had hung the corpses from the rooftop was standing between them and their big payday. This guy would interfere with their putting Kagan Trug in a hole, and if it was Boz Arcuri, as Makal said, then he could potentially have wired the entire warehouse with enough high explosives to take out the whole district.

"This is going to get messy," Gogin stated.

Makal pulled up in his jeep and got out. "Nice decorations."

"Arcuri?" Gogin asked. "If so, weren't his people covering this place?"

"Things have gotten complicated," Makal stated.

"How complicated?" Gogin inquired.

"Baydur gave me the green light to go balls to the wall against Sengor and Stone," Makal stated.

Gogin's eyes bugged. "You're shitting me."

"Nope. He said to bury this problem, or he'll bury me. Chances are, if we screw this up, you'll be sharing a grave with me, so keep your eyes open, all of you," Makal warned. "Arcuri's alone, but someone crazy enough to do that to his partners is crazy enough to take us out too."

Gogin's eyes clenched shut. "Great. Arcuri, Stone and Sengor too? How the hell did he get on the bad guys' side?"

"Since he's been ratting us out to Interpol," Makal growled.

Gogin leaned against the hood of one of the pickups, his legs feeling rubbery. "Interpol is onto us?"

"If they had warrants, Baydur wouldn't have given me the go-ahead to shut down Lem and the snoop he's working with," Makal stated. "I think the Interpol thing is a smoke screen for Stone. A fake identity to buy him some time to snoop around in other people's business."

Gogin nodded. "And if we kill them all, our problems go away?"

"Arcuri, Stone, Sengor and Trug. It's going to be a busy, bloody night," Makal explained.

"Trug too…great." Gogin picked up his rifle and checked the load in it. "This is a twisted path you led me on, Yuli."

"We clean out the worst of the Kurds, we put some trouble-makers in the ground, and we make a profit. Of course we're risking a lot, but we're also gaining a lot."

Makal locked and loaded his G-3 and advanced toward the warehouse.

Gogin shrugged and motioned for the other Jandarma enforcers to follow along.

He knew the sooner this was over with, the better.

Boz Arcuri, perched in the darkness of the rafters, saw the Jandarma team show up through a skylight window. Despite trying to keep a low profile, there wasn't much that they could do. They needed the big and obvious pickup trucks to take their skim away from the warehouse.

Arcuri sneered. He had submachine guns and assault rifles hidden in a pattern all over the warehouse, places he could find easily, in case one of his current weapons jammed or ran out of bullets. With the collection of firepower he'd assembled, he would be able to hold off the armies of hell should they come to his doorstep.

Something moved in the darkness below, slowly and quietly. It was the hint of a shadow, and it barely made a sound. Arcuri perched and waited. Whoever was down there was moving like a professional, and only the briefest of glimpses from the Kurd's vantage point had allowed him even that much. He smirked.

It had to have been Stone. Makal was a skilled veteran, but the wraith in black was more. There was a difference.

Outside the skylight, Arcuri caught the flash of headlights in the distance. Trucks, at least three of them, rolled down the street toward the warehouse. Even at this range, they were noisy and blatant. At least the Jandarma had pulled their vehicles into hiding, so no one else would catch sight of them from the road.

This had to be Kagan Trug's gambit.

The crusader. The hard-nosed cop. And the terrorist Kongra-Gel commander.

A mythic professional. A capable vigilante. And Trug...or whatever nest of incompetent psychotics that were in his service.

Arcuri grinned.

This might actually be enjoyable.

WHEN ABOOD OPENED her eyes, she was alone, her only company the glowing red LEDs on packets of explosives circling her. They still reminded her of cartoon images of rats in the shadows, their beady red eyes glowing with hateful malevolence. Abood winced as she turned her head. Her jaw throbbed painfully, but the pain cleared out her nightmare fantasy.

She had projected the evil of Boz Arcuri onto his deadly devices.

Abood tested the bonds at her back. Her wrists were tied together tightly, the coarse fibers of the rope digging into her skin. Any effort compounded the ache of her gunshot wound, though the cauterization that Arcuri had applied kept her from bleeding as she struggled. It wasn't going to be easy getting out of this mess, and even if she did, the warehouse was probably a maze of trip wires.

No, Abood thought. It wouldn't be a maze. Arcuri wanted to see Stone at ground zero.

She tried to spit out the foul taste of her mixed blood and

bile, but her mouth was too dry to do it. That was okay. She didn't even have enough in her stomach to gag up.

Welcome to our story, she thought. Catherine Abood and the really fucking painful day, already in progress.

She gritted her teeth and started to struggle with her wrist bonds, but then the jolting liquid fire of her broken jaw snapped her concentration and she almost blacked out. Abood rolled her head back upright and took in a deep breath. "Not good," she mumbled.

There was a racket outside, and she turned her head achingly. She was in an office, and outside the windows of the little open-top prefab room, she could see slivers of light opening up at the far end of the warehouse. Loading dock doors rolled up, and trucks lurched into the brief pools of illumination.

Found the supplies at least, she thought. Now if Stone shows up, kills all the bad guys, and defuses the high explosives…

Abood lowered her head. That was asking a lot. Even if Stone happened to be some legendary warrior, the odds were too long, especially with the psychotic Arcuri hidden somewhere in the shadows.

It might have been Makal, but Abood dismissed the blatant approach. Whoever was coming in acted like they owned the joint, and she doubted that the Jandarma, as crooked as it was, had enough forces available to bring in two huge trucks and crews to start loading supplies. No, this madness was probably the Kongra-Gel, stumbling into the middle of Arcuri's private vendetta.

Though, considering what she could remember from Arcuri's conversation with Kagan Trug over the phone, neither side seemed enamored of each other anymore. Maybe the army Trug sent was not just to load contraband, but to hunt down and kill whoever would try to stake a claim on the Kongra-Gel's ill-gotten gains.

Bullets, and planted explosives.

Hardly the loveliest of mixes. She remembered that C-4 wouldn't go off even if a bullet struck it, but if a detonator were to be hit, all bets would be off. And Arcuri, if he felt as if he was on the losing end, would end up triggering his dead-man switch. While that would truly ruin Abood's day, it would also destroy the medical supplies and whoever was in the warehouse.

If it was the Kurdish insurgents, that wouldn't be much of a loss. If it was Makal and his strike force, again, the world would be a better place.

But with the loss of a man like Brandon Stone...

Abood took another deep breath when she heard the floor creak behind her.

A hand clamped over her mouth, and pain seared through her skull. She had to have been getting used to it, because she didn't lose consciousness. Instead, she sat ramrod still and gritted through the pain in her jaw.

"Sorry I took so long," a familiar voice whispered in her ear.

Abood turned her head as far as she could. She sighed with relief.

"Boz...dead-man switch," Abood sputtered softly.

Brandon Stone glanced out over the warehouse. He then looked back at her and tilted his head. In the faint, dying light, something clicked in his eyes. "He broke your jaw. I'm sorry about—"

"Never mind," Abood cut him off. "A dead-man switch."

Stone nodded. "It's all I need to know," he said as he quickly began defusing the small packets of explosives around her, removing their detonators. After a moment of examination, he shook his head and placed them softly in a waste basket, after removing the detonators.

"Sengor..."

The blond Jandarma man who had been part of Makal's group stepped out of her peripheral vision, and her wrists were free now.

"Can you walk?" Sengor asked.

"Can try," Abood whispered. She got up, and though her knees wobbled, she managed to stay upright.

"The two of you pull out," Stone ordered. "Lem. Take her out the way we came in."

"But…" Sengor began.

"She's hurt badly, and she needs protection."

Sengor took a deep breath through his nose, lips pursed tightly. As Abood leaned against him, though, his unwillingness to follow orders disappeared.

"I've got it," Stone promised. "Keep her safe."

Sengor nodded. He slipped an arm under her shoulders and braced her.

Abood glanced back at the man she knew as Colonel Brandon Stone.

She hoped he'd make it out of this damned warehouse so she could see him again, and thank him.

Slowly, but surely, as she got out of the warehouse, she began recovering her ability to walk. She wished it was more.

Abood wanted to be in on this final fight.

A SEVEN-NATION ARMY couldn't stop the Executioner now. Between Makal, Trug's forces and Boz Arcuri, though, Mack Bolan had enough on his plate, but after nearly twenty-four hours of chasing after the murderers of relief workers, saving Turkish civilians and uncovering corrupt cells of Turkish security forces, he was ready to do what he did best.

Bolan had warmed up, delivering knockout punches to Kagan Trug's Kongra-Gel operations around Van. He'd struck quickly, but the firefight he watched building up around the warehouse was going to take every ounce of skill that he could muster. The Kurdish terrorists were the least of Bolan's worries, as far as enemy marksmen were concerned. Makal's Jandarma men had the better weapons, and presumably superior training and skill.

And there was Arcuri. While the man had proved capable of destroying a building and killing hundreds of people in one bomb blast, his skill at arms wasn't necessarily a match. However, considering the two slaughtered Kurdish sentries outside, Arcuri had far more on his side than simple marksmanship.

Bolan looked through the shadows, seeking possible hiding places. He glanced upward and saw a lump shift in the rafters.

The Executioner narrowed his eyes. Arcuri had a good view of the battlefield, and was probably hedging his bets. Let Bolan and Makal take out each other and the Kongra-Gel competition. And if anyone managed to catch sight of him, and was lucky enough to kill the insane Kurd, then he'd release the dead-man switch and the warehouse would be leveled.

Bolan had come too far across an earthquake and war-ravaged city to let the medical supplies be destroyed. He'd seen firsthand the people who needed him to succeed at stopping the loss of their relief supplies. Once Baydur coordinated the American and Turkish military forces to recover the stolen loot, thousands of wounded would have a chance to recover.

Bolan just had to take out Arcuri.

U.S. forces were in the area, according to Baydur. They had communications, which meant that the cell-phone usage had been restored by a forward command and control aircraft from the carrier that had sent relief troops.

The dead-man switch would only work if it had a proper radio signal.

The Executioner needed to stop that signal. It was the only way to put Arcuri down without risking the supplies in the warehouse. Anything else, even hand-to-hand combat, would be too much of a risk. Bolan opened his satellite phone. He had a clear signal.

He hoped that Stony Man Farm was listening.

When he heard Barbara Price's voice call him "Striker," Bolan couldn't help but smile at the one bit of luck he had that day.

Stony Man Farm, Virginia

THE UPLINK OF BOLAN'S satellite phone, relayed from the U.S. Navy's command and control frequencies, had Barbara Price on the line with him in an instant.

"Striker?"

"Can't talk much," Bolan answered. "Too many eyes and ears around me."

"We've got a location. His phone's GPS is transmitting," Akira Tokaido spoke up.

"Slaving a Keyhole satellite to our monitors," Carmen Delahunt announced. "Focusing infrared scanners on Striker's location."

"Good," Price replied. "We've got our eyes on you, Striker."

"I need a jamming signal to cut off this warehouse," Bolan explained.

"How thorough?" Huntington Wethers asked. "I'm working into the electronic warfare systems of the Navy C and C craft."

"I'm dealing with a maniac in control of a dead-man switch," Bolan told them. "I need a total shut down of all radio communications. Even the sat-phone signal."

Price winced. "We won't be able to give you a heads-up about how many bad guys are in the area."

"I've got enough intel here on the ground," Bolan said. "Cut this place off."

Price looked to Wethers, who nodded. "All right, Striker. Be careful."

Bolan killed his phone even as the signal dissolved into an indecipherable howl.

"How much opposition does Striker have on the ground?" Price asked.

Delahunt looked up from her monitor. "At least two groups. One of eleven. There's another thirty that came with the transport trucks. Two people are moving away from the warehouse now. One looks wounded according to how they're walking."

"Give me a close-up on those two," Price said. "Anything else I should be aware of?"

"There's someone else in the warehouse with Striker. Another solo party. From his infrared signature, he seems to be about forty or fifty feet off the floor," Delahunt explained. "Probably in the rafters."

"And probably the one holding on to the dead-man switch," Wethers commented.

"How come things are never straightforward," Price murmured.

Tokaido looked at his screen. "Looks straightforward enough to me. Striker just has to kill forty-two armed killers."

"And the smaller group of bad guys seems to be avoiding the larger group, sneaking into position to ambush them," Delahunt noted.

"Multiple disparate factions will make the odds better for Striker," Wethers said. "He's used such tactics before."

"So, it all comes down to one simple plan," Tokaido said. "Kill the bad guys and live."

Price nodded. "And Mack is an expert at that. But even he might be in over his head."

"We've got gunfire!" Delahunt shouted.

On the infrared monitor, stars winked in the warehouse.

The battle exploded to life, and the Executioner was in the middle of it.

AS SOON AS BOLAN TURNED off his satellite phone, he pocketed it and drew both of his Walthers. Thumbing back both hammers, he knew that the quiet pistols would give him an advantage in the opening round of this death struggle. There were too many enemies for him to take out more than one or two before he attracted a round of attention he couldn't avoid.

He sidestepped out onto a catwalk and crouched low. The muzzle-flash of the G-3 would be akin to wearing a neon target on his back. In the shadows, he had the advantage of stealth, and the Walthers' suppressors would swallow the fire the handguns would spit. The .380s were technically bigger than the HK's round, at least in cross section, but they didn't sit on a full-powered rifle charge. They weren't the ultimate in stopping power, and were weaker than anything Bolan regularly used. But he wasn't going for kills off the bat.

His aim was mayhem.

The Walthers hissed. The sound was barely louder than a polite cough, but at the other end of Bolan's line of fire, Kurdish insurgents jerked in pain as the pistol rounds smacked into their flesh. One of the Executioner's initial targets slammed hard against the fender of a truck, and slumped lifelessly to the ground, a lucky hit at that extreme range. Another gunner howled as he clutched a bleeding chest wound.

Bolan's brass fell chiming down the metal steps, drawing the attention of Makal's hidden Jandarma strike team. They turned and saw him beside the open office door, and were torn between gunning him down, and diving for cover as the Kongra-Gel force suddenly cut loose with blistering waves of automatic rifle fire.

Blazing stars of fire awoke at the other end of the warehouse, and Makal cursed, his rifle slicing the air that the Executioner had just evacuated. Bolan tucked his head and rolled down the steps, absorbing the impact of steel stairs on the powerful muscles of his shoulders and back instead of his head and neck. He came out of the roll, Walthers spitting suppressed slugs until they clicked empty.

Bolan didn't consider a reload, letting the quiet guns drop to the wayside.

It was time to get loud, now that the warehouse had become a war zone.

The Executioner swung his rifle into action, flicked off the safety and unleashed an earthshaking blast of autofire.

LEM SENGOR HEARD the beginning of the war behind him, the sudden ripping to life of AK-47s, sounding like the snap and crackle of demon wings as an army of devils took flight. He gripped his G-3 a little tighter, and was tempted to run back and give Brandon Stone some assistance. Only the soft weight resting on his shoulder—Catherine Abood—made him keep plowing forward, putting distance between himself and the warehouse.

Abood was showing signs of more strength, her second wind recovered, but Sengor couldn't leave her alone, not now. Her jaw was broken, and she'd lost too much blood. Her arm hung useless at her side. Even if she could hold a gun, she wouldn't be able to reload quickly, and anyone attacking her would have an easy time of killing or capturing her.

Sengor's face twisted in self-disgust. Stone had driven him off because the mysterious warrior knew full well that he wasn't up to the challenge of fighting the combined forces of the renegade Kurds and Turks.

Sengor put one foot in front of the other, holding Abood up, shielding her, scanning for trouble.

"Sengor," Abood hissed.

The blond Jandarma soldier turned to look at her, his G-3 raised like an oversized pistol.

Headlights glided toward them in the shadows of the warehouse district.

Sengor pulled Abood aside, taking cover behind a row of heavy wooden crates. It was another pickup truck, this one packed with riflemen. At the center of the truck bed stood

Kagan Trug, his face a mask of rage. He held a radio to his ear, shaking it as it was unresponsive.

"He's closing the door on a trap," Sengor hissed as he spotted another pickup truck trailing behind the first war wagon.

The vehicles stopped and Sengor could count another dozen men, armed with an assortment of deadly weapons. Trug himself carried an M-16/M-203, a combination of a rifle and grenade launcher. Sengor also spotted RPK light machine guns and HK machine guns.

"Hurry up," Trug ordered.

The machine gunners extended the bipods on their heavy weapons while the Kongra-Gel commander fed a 40 mm shell into the breech of his weapon.

The walls of the warehouse were sturdy, but against the power of machine guns, they might as well have been made of tissue paper. The grenade launcher was going to throw more of a nightmare into the mix.

"Gotta do sumfin," Abood grumbled, her broken jaw forcing her to slur her words. "Gun—"

Sengor glanced at her in disbelief, but she managed to struggle to her feet, supporting her own weight. "You're hurt," he said.

"Haffa break 'em up," Abood said.

Sengor nodded. He reached down and pulled out his Walther P-38 and handed it to her.

Abood tucked it under her injured arm, then held out her hand. "Mags."

Sengor handed her three of them, and she nodded. "Hold your fire until I can flank them," he said.

"Hurry," Abood told him.

Lem Sengor didn't need to be told twice. He dashed to the far side of the road, staying to the shadows, hoping that Trug's murderers would hold their fire until he got into position.

19

Makal looked up as he heard the tinkle of empty brass bouncing on steel. In the same moment, he heard the scream of pain and alert from the Kurds who'd pulled their trucks into the warehouse. At the top of the steps, near an open-topped office, he spotted a shadow in black, holding two handguns.

Makal sneered angrily. "Stone."

He swung up his G-3 and triggered it, but by the time he had brought the muzzle on target, the wraith in black tumbled down the stairs in a somersault. Makal had only plugged holes in empty air, and .380 slugs sparked all around him. One struck the Jandarma captain in his body armor, and Makal dived out of the way.

Assault rifles ripped to life at the other end of the warehouse, bullets sizzling through the air toward Makal and his team. He was glad he'd taken cover behind a couple of crates, even as bullets slammed into the wood.

It was a sucker play, Makal realized. Stone had started the battle, ruining his team's element of surprise. Somewhere in the darkness of the rafters, another muzzle-flash blazed, raining down fire.

Stone wasn't alone, and Makal figured that the freak in the rafters was none other than Boz Arcuri.

"When it rains, it pours," Makal hissed as he snaked between rows of crates.

The rest of his strike team had been separated, and he wasn't certain which of his partners were dead or alive. Stone's rounds hadn't cut through Makal's body armor, but someone could have caught a bullet in the head. As far as he was concerned, he was on his own. Other G-3s ripped into thunderous action, and Makal spotted a pair of Kurds rushing down an aisle up ahead.

Makal leveled his HK and triggered it, slamming a swarm of 7.62 mm NATO slugs into the two of them. Rifle bullets destroyed flesh and bone and threw two Kurdish corpses to the concrete floor like rag dolls. Gunfire ripped toward him, a couple of bullets socking the concrete near him. The Jandarma captain rolled to one side, getting out of the way of Arcuri's sniper assault.

Mass confusion reigned in the warehouse as warring parties cut into each other. Makal came around another crate, hoping to get a line of sight on Arcuri when something bounced into the middle of the floor.

White light and thunder blinded and deafened Makal.

BOZ ARCURI STOOD IN THE RAFTERS and drained his rifles into the squirming mass of panicked Kongra-Gel cannon fodder below him. With an AK-47 in each fist, he was able to hose sixty rounds into the hapless targets that scrambled for cover beneath him. It was like shooting fish in a barrel, and the rip and roar of his weapons drowned out Arcuri's manic laughter.

When the rifles emptied, he simply let them go, gravity pulling them from his hands, dozens of feet down to the floor. Arcuri jumped to another girder and scrambled toward his next supply of rifles. In the interim, he had a Browning Hi-Power out and cracking off shots at lightning speed. He spotted movement among Makal's forces and turned his attention to them, punching out nine shots to welcome them to his party.

The dead-man switch had been abandoned when its LED pulse turned to a single fiery glow. Its radio signal had been snuffed by some outside force, taking away his ace in the hole.

It didn't matter, Arcuri thought, his jaw clenched as he reloaded the Browning and emptied another 13-shot magazine toward Makal's crew. Bullets pinged on the steel around him, but he had the cloak of shadows and confusion, deflecting enemy gunfire as if the slugs were whisked aside by the hand of a god of vengeance.

Stone and Makal's and Trug's men were torn between multiple enemy targets. No one could concentrate on a single shadowy figure they could barely follow in the darkness. Not with dozens of other enemy guns focused on them. Arcuri laughed and scooped up another AK and patted the chest of a corpse.

"Go visit with your friends," Arcuri said to the dead man and he yanked a string of pins out of a half-dozen grenades taped to its chest. A hard kick sent the corpse to the ground at high speed. "Tell them Boz Arcuri sent you!"

The corpse exploded, fire, shrapnel and concussion waves bleeding off the shredded figure as fragmentation and stun grenades detonated in unison. Whoever wasn't torn to shreds by a sheet of high velocity, fragmented wire was left numbed and insensate by the brilliant flash of the stunners.

Crates were thrown around and cracked; gunmen below were howling in shock.

Arcuri triggered his AK into two stumbling gunmen. Jandarma thugs, he thought, by the looks of their armament and body armor. It didn't really matter who his targets were. Everyone below him was going to die, sent to hell to announce his impending arrival. The halls of the damned would swell with the souls of these rotten, petty pawns, and when Arcuri arrived, he would spit in the devil's eye and claim his very own corner of Hades, served for eternity by the scum he tore from life.

The AK-47 thundered almost as fast as Arcuri's heart, the Kurd's rage turned to fire and lead and launched at supersonic speeds to the mewling, confused weaklings beneath him.

"Die! Die for me!" Arcuri shouted as the rifle emptied and he reached for another weapon. "Die all of you!"

CATHERINE ABOOD BRACED against a fifty-five-gallon drum and thumbed back the hammer of the P-38 in her hand. Her father had always taught that shooting double action was no impediment, and indeed, she was a crack shot with a heavy trigger pull. However, Abood's strength was at a low ebb, and fighting fifteen pounds of pressure to crank off a single bullet would only result in wasted ammunition and the loss of her element of surprise. Hurt and exhausted, she knew that the light single action of the Walther would let her put a bullet into the head of whoever she aimed at.

A dozen men, armed with some of the heaviest hardware she'd seen since she'd toured a military base, readied themselves to slaughter everyone in the warehouse. All she had was the element of surprise and the need to be as ruthless as possible. It was hard, mentally, and her throat once more was sour with bile. Part of it was her upbringing, but it was also a moment of piercing, cold fear that told her that the assembled terrorists and their heavy weapons could easily turn her into a sack of hamburger with all that firepower.

Cold logic beat back the fear and dread. There were fifteen of them, and they intended to murder Brandon. Kill them and save his life.

Her index finger flexed against the trigger in anticipation of Lem Sengor's opening shot. She had the back of a machine gunner's head obscured by the front sight blade of the Walther. At this range, the 9 mm bullet would crush the base of the thug's skull and turn his brain into a mess of whipped soup.

Sengor's rifle cracked to life, shots exploding across the

rank of braced machine gunners. Abood dropped the hammer and her target's head detonated in a halo of blood. She swung on another of the gunmen. Their weapons ripped to life, bullets tearing at the warehouse in wild panic fire.

One of the Kongra-Gel killers rolled onto his back, RPK machine gun tracking toward Sengor, but Abood tripped the trigger three times, perforating the Kurdish terrorist's heart and lungs with full-metal-jacket slugs. The RPK erupted as the dying Kurd jerked the trigger in death, bullets wildly arcing into the sky.

Kagan Trug, the man with the M-16/M-203, and a few of the other men with regular assault rifles and grenade launchers, broke and ran for cover, their weapons chopping blindly into the shadows. One bullet bounced off Abood's drum and she sidestepped, kneeling down behind a crate. More projectiles chopped into the drum and the crate she crouched behind, metal parting and wood splintering. Still, nothing touched her. She returned fire, emptying the rest of the Walther into one of the riflemen. He collapsed, his back peppered with slugs.

Abood stuffed the narrow barrel of the handgun into the waistband of her jeans, and she pinched back the heel-release for the Walther's magazine. With a flick of her finger, she dragged the empty out of the handgun and tossed it aside. She fished a full stick of 9 mm slugs out of her pocket, and pushed it into the butt of the pistol, thanking her dad for teaching her how to reload with one hand. She snaked the Walther out of her waistband, tripped the slide release with her index finger, and the Walther's action closed, stripping the first live round and loading it into the barrel.

"Come get some," Abood growled as she triggered the pistol again, catching a machine gunner in the face as he struggled to swing around his massive weapon.

All doubts had left her, and her exhaustion disappeared behind a flood of adrenaline.

The only things that were left in her mind were the will to fight, and the skill to back it up.

MACK BOLAN SLITHERED into the open to get the drop on a pair of Jandarma enforcers who were busily cutting down the ranks of the Kongra-Gel thugs. He was about to pull the trigger on his HK when he saw something drop from the rafters.

Instinct honed on countless battlefields took over, and the Executioner lunged for the cover of a crate. Instants later, his gut reaction was rewarded with the thundering cacophony of a half-dozen grenades detonating at once. Bolan had screamed as he saw the body falling, not in fear, but to equalize the pressure in his eardrums. Facing the floor, he saw his head cast in shadow from the eruption of several flash-bang grenades. The thunderclap that accompanied the man-made lightning would have deafened him if he hadn't armored his hearing with the yell.

Bolan rose to his feet and scanned the rafters to see Arcuri cut loose with his rifle. The weapon's muzzle-flash lit the Kurdish madman's face, and he could see that the terrorist was laughing as he blazed away against the Jandarma riflemen on the ground. The Executioner was one pull of the trigger away from ending Arcuri's menace forever when someone leaped off the top of a crate and dropped onto him.

The Executioner's rifle was knocked from his grasp, the combined weight of two men crashing hard into the concrete floor. With a surge of strength, Bolan twisted and hurled his attacker off his back. It took an instant for him to figure out what stung his eyes, making it hard to see in the darkness, but then he identified his impairment. The man who jumped him was a bloody mess, and Bolan had been splashed in the eyes.

He wiped away the gore, blinking his vision back to normal when the wounded man lurched forward again, screaming in half-blind rage. The Executioner saw the thug, holding a knife in his one good hand, the remaining hand and half of the attacker's face stripped away by shrapnel. Bolan concentrated on the knife and deflected the monstrosity's first swing with his wrist. Forearm blocked forearm, and the warrior grabbed the knife fighter's elbow. With a twist, Bolan had his enemy's blade arm trapped. The wounded Turk howled and sputtered, spit and blood spraying in the big soldier's face, but Bolan clenched his eyes shut against the blinding mist.

The Executioner turned at the waist, and bone snapped as he dislocated the knife man's shoulder and elbow in one savage turn of his body. The wounded killer flipped across Bolan's hip and crashed face-first into the ground. Bolan finished him off with a hard stomp to the base of the Turk's neck, vertebrae crunching under two-hundred-plus pounds of force. The faceless attacker shuddered once, and was still.

Bolan reached down and pulled out his USP Compact, rather than hunt for the rifle he'd lost moments before. Arcuri shouted something in Kurdish, but from the tone, it could have been any insane gibberish spouted by a man shoved over the edge. Bolan swung up the pistol and fired twice, but Arcuri leaped to another girder, sparks flashing on the ceiling in the madman's wake.

Luck was still with the Kurdish psychopath, and Bolan was forced to duck behind a crate as rifle fire erupted to his left. Enemy bullets sought him, and the Executioner returned fire, catching the gunman with three shots. His pistol cut down the enemy, and Bolan raced toward the tumbling corpse in hopes of scrounging a new rifle to keep him in the wild melee around him.

That's when the wall to one side suddenly sprouted dozens of holes, heavy machine-gun fire cutting into the warehouse.

Bolan hit the floor under the wave of high-powered bullets.

Someone else had just joined the party, and the Executioner suddenly worried about the safety of Catherine Abood and Lem Sengor.

The free-for-all only grew more complicated, and Bolan continued toward the fallen gunman he'd just killed, knowing that the doomsday numbers had built into an avalanche. And he was in its deadly path.

Stony Man Farm, Virginia

BARBARA PRICE WATCHED the newcomers move in on the warehouse. Two truckloads—nearly twenty men—divided between the two vehicles, set up in a skirmish line that would allow them to cover the warehouse. Price's stomach turned as she saw the back door slam on a death trap. Inside the warehouse, muzzle-flashes burned brightly on the infrared image, and bodies quickly began to cool to room temperature.

The number of living inside the building dropped quickly as gunmen waged vicious war.

Then, in the center of the warehouse, a brilliant sun came into being.

"What was that?" Price asked.

"Grenades going off, several of them," Wethers answered. "The man in the rafters is trying to level the playing field."

Price stood, tense, watching the chaos. "Can we get a message to Striker about the skirmish line outside?" she asked.

"No," Delahunt said. "We're jamming on all frequencies, and his hands are full."

"We've got tactical movement outside," Tokaido announced. "Someone's flanking the newcomers."

Price nodded. She remembered the name of the Jandarma operative Bolan had claimed was helping Interpol, probably just an honest soldier he'd rescued from moral quandaries or mortal perils. "Sengor and Abood, probably," she guessed.

"The smaller one, Abood, I guess, looks pretty shaky," Tokaido told her. "But they're in position for an ambush."

Price scanned the screen, and Tokaido helped her by enlarging the image of the skirmish line, its magnification reduced so that she could see where Bolan's two allies had come in behind the gunners. Their weapons erupted to life, and the assembled gunmen jerked in reaction to bullets crashing through their bodies.

"The sniper in the rafters doesn't appear to have the deadman trigger with him," Wethers announced. "We can't kill the jamming now, its transmitter is wide open."

Price's lips pulled into thin, bloodless lines around her mouth. "There's no way to drop information to Striker."

"I'm trying to narrow it down," Aaron Kurtzman announced.

Price was startled. She'd expected him to be sleeping after a day of coordination efforts. Bolan in harm's way, though, had a way of bringing the wheelchair-bound genius to full alert, even without the monstrous coffee he brewed.

"Not that Striker will have time to chat on the phone, but—"

"Just do it," Price ordered.

"It's a simple process," Tokaido said. "There's only a narrow band of wavelengths that these transmitters can operate on. The trouble is narrowing it down to a single band without spraying interference across nearby communication bands."

"And clearing it up means narrowing it down to only one frequency," Kurtzman responded. "It'll be tight, and it'll take a few minutes, and by then—"

"The fight will be over," Price said.

"I'd use a variation on Gadgets Schwarz's transmitter killer pulse, but the same frequency would also fry the detonators on the explosives in the warehouse," Kurtzman explained. "Killing the transmitter would also activate the bombs."

"Unless..." Price began. "How focused can we direct the radio beam?"

Kurtzman's eyes narrowed. "With laser precision if we have a target."

"Carmen, have you been tracking the progress of the guy in the rafters?" Price asked.

"I've got him on video and digital playback," Delahunt replied. The ex-FBI computer expert was hit by recognition. "Rewinding!"

"Of course, he probably ditched the trigger the moment we started jamming on all frequencies," Kurtzman responded. "And once we figure out where he threw the trigger…"

"Blast it with a tight focus beam," Price concluded.

"Working on it!" Kurtzman responded.

Price hoped that they could find the transmitter in time.

THE EXECUTIONER VAULTED over another crate as he spotted Makal in retreat. The Turk's G-3 blazed a fireball of devastation, heavy rifle slugs sizzling through the air close enough for Bolan to feel their heat. The soldier triggered the AK-47 he'd grabbed off a dead Kurd and ripped off half a magazine, but Makal was as slippery as ever, disappearing behind a pillar and down an aisle of stacked boxes. Bolan cursed at his luck in not catching the corrupt Jandarma captain.

Instead, Bolan dropped to the floor as Arcuri's sniper fire homed in on him again. The Executioner pivoted and fired off a quick burst at the Kurd before more Kongra-Gel thugs stumbled around a corner. Too close for him to swing around the muzzle, Bolan charged into them, using his elbows and the steel folding stock as his weapons.

The Executioner started the conflict with a crash of steel off one Kurd's cheek. The insurgent's head twisted at an unnatural angle, and he fell into one of his compatriots. As bullets chopped the floor behind him, Bolan dived in and caught a terrorist in the throat with a wicked elbow strike. The blow crushed the Kurd's windpipe, and he gagged and sputtered. Bolan hauled around the assault rifle, and used its steel frame to hook the choking man as a shield. Rifle slugs made the dying gunman jerk violently, but his body stopped them before they could touch the warrior.

The second Kurdish killer tossed his stunned friend aside and lunged at the Executioner. Instead of getting handfuls of Bolan's combat suit, he received a face full of the big man's elbow. Stopped cold, the attacker lost his momentum. Bolan snaked his arm back and around the Kurd's neck and wrenched him in close. Caught in a headlock, the stunned terrorist served as a fulcrum so that Bolan could run up the side of a crate and kick off.

The Executioner's flying weight was too much for the stunned insurgent. Leverage ground the trapped terrorist's neck bones to powder, and his spine was torn out of his brain by the root. Skin and muscle held the head to his shoulders in a limp, stringy mess as Bolan released the corpse and landed on the ground in a crouch.

Arcuri's sniper fire swung wildly to reach Bolan, but he'd taken himself out of the maniac's path. Bolan wondered at what happened to the heavy machine-gun fire that had torn through the wall a few moments ago. Whatever happened, it was over, for now, and he tried not to think about Sengor and Abood battling it out with heavily armed thugs.

That's when he saw the thing sitting on the floor, red LED lights glowed. It was shaped like a dumbbell, except with radio components at either end.

The dead-man switch!

The Executioner knew that if he could disable the device, then he could get back in touch with Stony Man Farm once he got to some cover. All it would take would be a mad dash across the open floor. No enemies loomed in his peripheral vision, but Arcuri was still in action up in the rafters. Bolan took a cue from the Kurdish bomber and plucked a grenade from his harness.

He took out a length of cord, wrapped it around the detonator of a flash-bang and plucked the pin. With two hard spins on the end of the line, he had enough force to hurl the bomb up and into the rafters. As it reached the zenith of its arc, it detonated.

A blaze of light filled the air in the ceiling, and a rifle tumbled from the rafters.

Bolan had his chance and he dashed toward the dead-man switch. In four long strides, he had it in hand. A moment later, something smashed into his chest with all the force of a sledgehammer. The Executioner looked up as he tumbled backward, the flare of a muzzle-flash dominating his vision.

20

Stony Man Farm

"Striker went for the detonator!" Kurtzman shouted as Delahunt swung the viewer toward where Arcuri had thrown his dead-man switch in a fit of frustration. The jamming had prevented the detonator from sending out its lethal signal, but in blanketing the warehouse with a wave of electronic countermeasures, the Stony Man cyberteam had cut off Mack Bolan from vital information about his enemy's movements.

Price watched the screen as if she could dive through and go to his aid.

Instead, she could only watch as a grenade flared in the warehouse and then Bolan's dash for the trigger.

He bent and scooped it up.

Price's heart rocketed into her throat as she saw a rifleman blast at the Executioner, his body tumbling.

"Mack…"

"Sengor and Abood are taking fire!" Akira announced.

"This is going to be one of those nights," Price murmured. She glanced back to where Bolan had been on the screen, and he was gone. She sucked in a deep breath. "Get in touch with Jandarma command. Striker needs backup now."

THE EXECUTIONER HIT the floor and rolled, his rifle still in hand. He tucked under the wheel of a truck and pulled the trigger. With only one hand controlling the weapon, it was a spray of wild shots at the gunner who'd fired on him. His chest ached, but he could still breathe. Bolan had taken shots to the chest before, and he knew the difference between a lethal hit and what he'd been subjected to. He discarded the AK and crawled, dead-man switch locked in his fist. He reached the other side of the truck and pulled his pistol.

He caught movement out of the corner of his eye and ducked back under the frame of the truck, avoiding decapitation by a stream of autofire. Bolan triggered the pistol between the wheels, and the blast of rifle slugs turned off track, bullets dancing on the concrete in a line away from the truck. The Executioner lunged out from under one vehicle and into the cab of a neighboring transport, moments before a renewed focus of assault-rifle fire tried to home in on him. The bullets rattled on the fender and door of the truck, but Bolan had snaked across the driver's seat.

Through the rear window of the cab, he caught sight of his target—it was Makal. Bolan hammered out two quick shots, but the Jandarma captain ducked behind the tailgate of the other transport. He poked his rifle out around the corner and cut loose with his G-3 in a Hail Mary move, firing without aiming. Bolan dropped back and heavy-caliber rifle rounds smashed through the seat backs, spitting rubber and shreds of leather. In the leg well of the cab, the Executioner was protected from the salvo of powerful bullets by the bulk of the seats, but the thin backs and the sheet metal of the cab were little impediment to the powerful rifle.

Bolan looked down at his chest and saw that one of the spare magazines for his own G-3 had been what stopped a glancing slug from smashing his chest open. He fed his pistol a spare magazine and pushed open the far door. When the passenger-side door rattled and jerked under an onslaught of slugs, the savvy soldier ducked back past the steering wheel and grabbed the side of the truck.

It would take only a few heartbeats for Makal to cut around after realizing he'd just missed Bolan, and the Executioner stuffed his handgun away. He ripped a grenade off his harness, popped the pin and rolled the bomb toward the rear fender. Bolan launched himself into the bed of the truck, the tailgate shielding him. The grenade, a stun-shock blaster, erupted with blinding and deafening force.

Makal staggered out into the loading dock, punching out more shots.

Bolan drew his pistol and snap-aimed at his lethal adversary, but a bullet smashed into the bed of the truck next to his knee. With a somersault, the warrior dodged out of the way as more slugs rained at the spot he'd just been.

Arcuri was still in the fight. Gunfire had died down back in the warehouse, the medical supplies standing silent amid a concrete floor spattered with blood and gore. Corpses were mute testimony to the raging war between Kurdish insurgents and Turkish racists. The animals, with a little help from the Executioner, had slaughtered each other, turning the storehouse into an abattoir. Bolan still had the dead-man switch in his fist and he needed to get rid of it, but not before he deactivated it. With the skirmish against Makal, and Arcuri's interference, he hadn't been able to take care of it yet.

Bolan leaped over the tailgate and landed on the floor, Arcuri's fire unable to reach him in the shadow of the heavy vehicle. He tore open the battery case and its cells ejected. The LEDs dimmed, lifeless, its coiled menace fading like a snake with its head sliced off. The Executioner hurled the empty device far into the loading dock, its electronic components shattering on sloped concrete.

Makal opened fire on the broken device, then he threw down his rifle in frustration.

The Turk was out of ammo, at least for the big HK. Bolan knew that Makal still wasn't helpless.

That's when he heard another grenade detonate outside of the warehouse.

Of the forces that had opened fire during the melee, at least one or two were still in the fight. The only ones that Bolan knew were outside to defend against the attackers were Sengor and Abood. Bolan cut through the loading dock door, Arcuri's pistol fire chasing his heels as he raced along.

Makal and the Kurdish mad bomber could wait for a moment. Bolan's allies needed help.

LEM SENGOR STRUGGLED to reload his rifle after he raked the Kongra-Gel gunners' ranks. While he was trained in the use of the rifle, he'd never needed more than one magazine at a time, and a speed reload was something that he'd not been trained in. Sengor usually fired on single shot, and twenty bullets, well-aimed, were enough for most of the fights he'd ever been in.

Now, he couldn't quite get his magazine seated into his rifle, and Kagan Trug cut loose with a burst from his M-16.

Sengor dived to one side, hypervelocity slugs sizzling in the air over his head. The G-3 was long lost, tossed aside in his mad dive to escape. Instead, the blond Jandarma lieutenant tumbled behind the cover of Trug's own pickup truck and grabbed his spare Walther PPK. A .380 against an assault rifle wasn't Sengor's idea of a fair fight, but it was all he had, and the compact handgun would have to do.

The M-16 stopped its chatter, and he heard the Kurd cursing a blue streak.

Sengor swung around the corner and leveled his pistol at the Kongra-Gel leader.

"Drop the weapon!" Sengor shouted.

Instead, Trug ducked behind one of his remaining riflemen. Sengor tried to tag him with a shot, and ended up coring the hapless PKK gunman with two shots, killing him instantly. Trug triggered the grenade launcher on his rifle instead.

Sengor watched the heavy shell float almost lazily past him, crashing against the wall of another warehouse, twenty feet behind him. The Jandarma lieutenant tried to run out of the blast radius, but the concussion wave picked him up and hurled him against the pickup's fender like a rag doll.

Stunned, Sengor slumped to the ground, body aching from head to toe.

Trug pulled out his handgun.

"What's it feel like to know you're about to die, half blood?" Trug asked, thumbing back the pistol's hammer.

Sengor looked at the Walther on the ground. He'd never be able to reach it in time, not to save his life, but if he could get it, he could at least take Trug with him.

Gunfire erupted before Sengor could act. Trug jerked as bloody wounds appeared on his arm. Trug cursed wildly, his gun dropped from numbed fingers. He growled and raced away down a side alley.

Sengor looked over his shoulder and saw Abood, gun held up in one hand, staggering toward him, her feet dragging with the effort to walk. She looked around, then, stuffing her pistol into her waistband, she fumbled a loaded magazine into it.

Sengor spotted another figure racing from the front of the warehouse, and he reached for his fallen handgun, but stopped when he heard his name called by a familiar voice. His vision refocused as he recovered from the grenade explosion, and he recognized the long, lean form of Brandon Stone.

Sengor let the gun rest in his lap and he looked at Abood, who leaned on the hood of the pickup.

"Thanks," he told her, his voice barely a croak.

Abood nodded, unable to speak, her jaw swollen and distorted now.

Bolan closed in on them and paused, checking behind him. He stopped when he reached a body with an RPK machine gun and he scooped it up, grabbing two spare 70-round drums to tuck into his battle harness. He checked the load in the weapon, and satisfied that it was ready to fight, he continued toward the pair.

"The Kongra-Gel?" Bolan asked.

"Trug," Sengor replied. "He took off after Abood shot him."

Bolan glanced to the reporter. She winked at him, then rested her forehead on a pillow formed by her wrists. Bolan helped the Jandarma man to his feet. "How healthy do you feel?"

Sengor gave the American a quizzical look. "I feel like I've been run over by a train."

"Can you drive?" Bolan asked.

Sengor nodded.

"Get in the pickup and head back to Baydur," Bolan ordered. "This place is still dangerous, and we need bomb disposal teams in here to clean—"

Bolan's satellite phone burbled, and he plucked it from his pocket.

"Yeah, the dead-man switch is dead. I took care of it. Otherwise, you wouldn't be calling me, right?" Bolan said into the phone. He glanced back at the warehouse, apparently concerned with other killers in the building. "You've got the satellite tracking them both? I just heard from Sengor that Trug is running away. I'd rather not wait."

Bolan looked to Sengor. "My people inform me that Baydur's already en route. Transport helicopters and trucks are heading in right now. If you stay put, you both can get medical assistance as soon as they arrive."

Sengor nodded. "Sounds safer than driving."

Bolan pocketed the satellite phone. "Stay put. Here, switch handguns. All I have are PPK magazines left."

"I'd feel a little safer with a full-power 9 mm anyway," Sengor admitted.

Bolan traded the USP Compact for Sengor's Walther, stuffing it in the empty holster he was wearing. It fit snugly.

Bolan gave Abood's shoulder a gentle touch. She nodded and stepped away from the pickup. As Bolan got into the cab, Sengor helped the tough reporter stand aside, gently supporting her with an arm.

Bolan slid behind the steering wheel and fired the truck to life.

The Executioner still had demons to hunt in the night.

Stony Man Farm, Virginia

BARBARA PRICE RELAYED information to Mack Bolan over the satellite phone link. The cyberteam had split its efforts, using enhanced imagery to track all three of the Executioner's targets as they split up, fleeing through the earthquake shattered city. Aaron Kurtzman, however, was on the line, posing as a U.S. Navy command and control officer, and guided Major Omar Baydur's forces toward the warehouse.

The full power of the cyberteam was in operation, and Price felt useful again.

Bolan had swung off after the escapee he identified as Kagan Trug. Trug had broken into a vehicle after running two blocks, and was driving through the streets. Wethers had identified it as a Volkswagen SUV, and it navigated the broken rubble more easily than the Toyota pickup that Bolan had snagged.

"He's got a three-block lead on you," Price said. "He's within rifle range."

"If I want to hose down civilians," Bolan answered. "Are the streets clear?"

"Hunt?" Price asked.

"Trug's the only warm body for five blocks," Wethers reported.

"That's all I need to hear," Bolan stated.

She watched the heat signature of the Toyota truck skid to a halt.

KAGAN TRUG LUNGED through the darkness as if the devil himself were hot on his heels. The whole mess had gone to hell, and Trug didn't want to get burned with the rest of his men. He didn't know if anyone else was still alive, and armed only with a tiny pocket-pistol, he wasn't about to sit and continue to fight, not when he had a compound and a dozen of the best armed guards the Kurdish People's Party could provide.

Let the exhausted avenger on his heels try to fight his way past them, even if he could trace Trug through the wrecked city. Trug stopped when he saw a parked open-topped Volkswagen. He climbed in and searched around, finding the keys to the vehicle in the ash tray. The Kurdish terrorist leader grinned, luck still smiling on him. He fired up the vehicle and gunned it into the road, thick knobby tires rolling over broken asphalt and cracked concrete with ease.

"Come on, come on," Trug goaded the vehicle, picking up speed. He glanced back and saw two headlights in the distance.

They burned with all the hatred of a demon's eyes. Trug stomped on the gas and the Volkswagen bounced wildly over the rubble. The VW skidded and slipped on chunks of smashed road and buildings. He swerved wildly back and forth while the hunter behind him kept in a straight line, hounding him, as if directed by spotters in heaven.

"Damn it, damn it!" Trug snapped, pounding at the steering wheel. The VW jammed its fender against a collapsed section of wall he didn't see. The vehicle struggled and he tried to buffalo past it. He cursed himself for paying more attention to his hunter, and not the road in front of him. He glanced back and saw that the headlights had stopped.

"Can't get past the road, eh?" Trug asked. He ground the transmission into reverse, but stone and bent metal were tangled completely. He couldn't get the VW to move.

The dashboard to his right suddenly exploded under a hail of heavy bullets. Trug froze in his seat, shocked at the sudden, almost whisper-silent assault on him. He recovered his senses and jerked violently forward, flame piercing his lungs. He bounced off the steering wheel and back into the seat. His chin dropped to his chest, and he saw his ribs poking through his jacket, blood flushing hotly into his lap.

Kagan Trug's lips moved, struggling to get out a final curse against the monster that had slain him, but the Kongra-Gel commander didn't even have the breath for that.

Instead, his lungs sputtered and bubbled blood out through gaping exit wounds in his chest.

Trug slumped in his seat, his eyes on the side mirror. Those burning demonic headlights turned away before oblivion claimed him.

"ONE DOWN," BOLAN announced over the satellite phone. "Where's Arcuri?"

"He disappeared off the satellite," Barbara Price informed him. "He got to ground level, and then he cut between two buildings. We lost his infrared signature."

"He took to the drainage systems in the docks," Bolan replied. "Even if some of the tunnels have collapsed, there's enough of a labyrinth down there that he can bypass any blockage."

"That's what we figured. Akira is bringing up whatever we can find on the tunnel system."

"What about Makal?" Bolan asked.

"He hooked up with another gunman and they picked up a vehicle. They're hightailing it out of there."

"Got a description?" Bolan asked.

"Another jeep. I'll direct you, since they'll be easier to track," Price said. "We can get Arcuri another day."

"Maybe another hour, but Arcuri isn't lasting another day," Bolan replied. "Steer me."

YULI MAKAL PUNCHED Gogin across the jaw to shut him up.

"I know we've blown it!" Makal snapped. "But what the hell are we going to do?"

Gogin wiped the blood from his lips and glared at the Jandarma captain. "I don't know. You're the one in charge. You're the one who should have anticipated we were going to run into major opposition at that damned warehouse."

Makal slid behind the wheel and fired up the engine. "Get in."

"Or what?" Gogin asked.

"Or I leave you for whoever is still fighting inside," Makal answered. "If you feel like staying here and stopping a bullet, be my guest."

Gogin scrambled into the passenger seat. "Where's your rifle?"

Makal's lips pulled into a grim crack across his face.

"You lost it?"

"I used up everything I had fighting in there. I notice you still have ammo," Makal growled as he pulled out. "Maybe you were hiding behind a crate instead of killing terrorists."

Gogin's glare seemed to pick up extra intensity. "Are you saying that I'm a coward?"

Makal sneered, then shook his head. "It was chaos in there. I couldn't see anyone half the time. They were throwing flash grenades and I was blind."

"So you just burned off everything when you couldn't see," Gogin answered.

"We have to pull back and get out of town."

"Leave?" Gogin asked.

Makal groaned. "Oh, sure, let's stay in town with the Kongra-Gel and Baydur on our backs, not to mention Stone."

"You have friends in the Jandarma command. They can look out for us. I'm not running away from my city. I have family and friends here," Gogin stated. "We went after the PKK and the Kongra-Gel like we did to drive *them* out. Now I'm an exile?"

Makal frowned. "I'm sorry…"

Gogin rolled his head back between his shoulders. "This is my home. I grew up here. I love this city, and instead of helping my neighbors, what am I stuck doing? Nursing a leg shot, and then trying to get more money in my pocket."

"You're going soft on me too?" Makal asked. "We were there to drop the sword on Trug's neck. He's dead, we get the medical supplies back and everything gets better. But we screwed up."

"Yeah. I screwed up, throwing in with you," Gogin stated. "I trusted you!"

Makal rolled his eyes and saw something flicker in the side mirror. "Oh God—"

Gogin looked back. "It could be anyone."

"I'm doing sixty kilometers an hour," Makal replied. "And he's closing in on us."

Gogin paled, his anger fading away. "Stone."

"We can discuss our problems later, we need to act like a team," Makal explained.

Gogin braced his rifle on the seat. "I grabbed ammo from some of the fallen while we were retreating. I wasn't being a coward. I just wanted to be able to fight."

"Just shoot Stone," Makal growled. "Kill him."

Gogin held down the trigger on the G-3. Bullets streaked through the night and sprayed the road behind them. The headlights swerved, then winked out. "He's driving without lights."

"Trying to keep you from homing in on him," Makal surmised.

"It isn't going to work. I catch glimpses of him," Gogin replied. He stuffed a fresh magazine into his rifle. "He's not getting away from me."

The weapon exploded to life again. Metal sparked, closer this time.

Makal swerved and cut down an alley, then hit the brakes after spinning out, blocking the path. "Come on!"

Makal pulled his CZ-75, and he and Gogin raced deeper into the shadows of the alley. "He'll see where we pulled in and he'll cut right after us."

"And then hit the jeep. Good plan," Gogin replied. He aimed the G-3 at the alley entrance. "And when he does..."

"We drop every bullet we have into him."

Gogin grinned. "Yeah. He stole our future, but we're ripping his from him."

Makal nodded. He had a sliver of hope left as he thumbed back the hammer on his pistol.

Stony Man Farm, Virginia

"STRIKER, YOU THERE?" Price asked.

"You're on speakerphone," Bolan answered. "What's wrong?"

"Makal turned off and stopped cold," she replied. "They're up to something."

"I've got it," Bolan returned. "Give me an alternate route in."

Price looked to Delahunt, who was busy tracking them.

"In the shadows of the buildings, we can't see where they're hiding," Delahunt explained. "But there seems to be a gap between two that leads to their alley."

"I see it, turning off," the Executioner returned. "Going EVA."

"Striker..." Price began. But there was no response, and Bolan's form disappeared into the shadow of the block. She chewed her lower lip, and knew that Bolan would be aware of the dangers of the unstable buildings, and the possibility that his route in would be blocked off. With the phone left in the truck, she wouldn't be able to keep track of his progress.

"Good luck," she whispered impotently.

THE EXECUTIONER ENTERED the gangway, the RPK light machine gun leading him, its barrel seeking enemies in the shadows. Bolan spent a moment, allowing his eyes to adjust to the few wisps of light visible in the alley. Ahead of him, piles of rubble and garbage would slow his approach, but Bolan was committed to his path. He slung the RPK, realizing that while its power was significant, he'd need maneuverability.

He braced his long arms against the walls of the gangway, planted one boot in the crease between bricks, and shoved himself higher up. Crab walking, he cleared overturned and crushed metal drums once used for garbage cans. Rubble had pounded and smashed them to pieces. Bolan glanced up and saw a hole had been torn in the wall by the earthquake, and after a quick scramble, he clawed his way to the bottom edge of the gaping wound in the wall.

It wasn't the most graceful of climbs, but he reached the lip and hauled himself into position. He risked his pocketlight for a moment, its bright LED bulb spraying the area in its sharp glow. Sections of floor were missing, and the drop to the levels below would guarantee a broken leg in the darkness. Weakened floorboards might allow him a safe passage. He adjusted the light to its minimum setting and gave himself a soft halo by which to see.

There was a window overlooking the alley where Makal and his ally had retreated.

If he could reach that without giving away his presence, he'd have the drop on the two Jandarma renegades.

And then he'd deliver the judgment they'd worked so hard to earn.

Bolan walked carefully, boots resting on wood, testing it with his weight, feeling for it to flex. Boards that held without a creak or a groan of protest were the ones he stood on as he felt for another length of floor that could support his weight.

He took another step and reached the edge of a hole. He looked down and saw Yuli Makal and Gogin behind the cover of a collapsed pile of bricks.

Bolan reached for his Walther and clicked off the light.

As the lens extinguished, Gogin turned his head.

The Jandarma rifleman swung his rifle around, shouting a warning to Makal.

Weapons exploded in the alley, and Bolan dived for cover, his body smashing through weakened floorboards. Bullets cut the air behind him as the Executioner tumbled out of control into the darkness.

21

Mack Bolan had fallen enough times to know how to land with minimal injury, but in the darkness, he couldn't see to steer his body. Limp, he bounced off a support beam and tumbled backward, his face smarting where he'd struck the pillar. Bolan twisted so he wouldn't land on the slung RPK, its wood and steel certain to snap his shoulder and break his ribs should he land on the weapon. Instead, Bolan flopped on the opposite side of his body.

The impact knocked the wind out of him, and he glanced up, one eye blinded by blood from a cut on his forehead. Makal swung his handgun at the Executioner, the CZ-75 cracking out a fast three 9 mm slugs. Bolan dived down the slope of rubble he'd just struck to avoid the gunfire. Sparks flew as copper-jacketed bullets, denied flesh, struck concrete.

Pain caught up with Bolan as he crab walked through the darkness, keeping his head under the savage gunfire that hunted him. He reached a section of wall that hid him from view, and he checked himself by touch.

Except for his forehead, he wasn't bleeding, and no broken bones were in evidence. Pulled and bruised muscles gave sparks of protest from his impact, but once again, Bolan's superb physical conditioning and agility had protected him from severe injury. He reached for the Walther in its holster and pulled it out.

He no longer felt the weight of the RPK hanging on his shoulder.

When Bolan smashed into the mound of rubble, the gun had to have gone one way while he tumbled in the other. He thumbed back the tiny pistol's hammer to give himself an easier trigger pull—accuracy was vital now that he had only the pistol and its .380-caliber payload.

He'd intended to use the pocket-pistol to ambush Makal and his ally, but without surprise to give him the accuracy to make up for his lack of power, he was going to need every ounce of skill and craft to get the job done.

The Executioner peered around a corner, his bloodied face obscuring his features in the shadows. Makal and Gogin scanned wildly about, asking each other if they'd seen any movement, or Bolan's corpse sprawled on the floor.

"Stone!" Makal shouted. "Stone! It doesn't have to end this way for you."

Bolan remained silent as he eased himself into the darkness, cradled to it as if they were old friends. In a way, they were, and it had shielded him countless times, giving him the advantage of surprise against hordes of enemies. Once more, the Executioner stalked like an invisible predator, stealth his greatest weapon.

Outnumbered and outgunned, battered by his fall and exhausted after a day of battling earthquakes, insurgents and crooked soldiers, Mack Bolan may have slowed down, but he was not going to make it easy for Makal and Gogin to kill him.

It won't end this way for me, the Executioner resolved.

YULI MAKAL FED HIS CZ-75 another stick, then pulled his P-38 backup pistol. He'd need firepower to take down Stone. One man had swept the tide of battle between the combined numbers of the Kongra-Gel thugs sent to pick up the medical supplies and Makal's own veteran team. The Jandarma captain had seen too many of his men slain by this man. Only Gogin's paranoid alertness had saved them from an ambush.

But now, the man was hidden in the shadows of a partially collapsed building. Makal wondered if he should use the flashlight in his pocket, but then he realized that the glowing bulb would only make him an easier target for his adversary. Makal pointed for Gogin to flank the hole and take up a firing position.

"Listen, we've already spoken," Makal said. "But you have the wrong impression of me. I'm not a bad man. I do what I do for the safety of my countrymen."

There was no answer, and Makal took a tentative step deeper into the darkness. His eyes adjusted to the dimmer light, and he saw a forest of rubble and destruction ahead of him that a small army could hide in. Makal wondered if it was a good idea, moving in to smoke the enemy out. Then he saw a faint glow.

Makal thumbed back the Walther's hammer and took careful aim, then paused. He glanced back to Gogin instead, and motioned for the Turk to hose the glow with a blast of heavy-caliber rifle fire. The captain stepped to one side, giving his partner a clear field of fire, then nodded for Gogin to cut loose.

As the G-3 erupted, 7.62 mm NATO slugs slicing through the inky blackness surrounding him, Makal raised both handguns, took a sidestep and crouched deeply, firing at floor level with both pistols. A hasty shot from the enemy cracked out, but Bolan was on the retreat, caught in a cross fire. The pathetic muzzle-flash of Bolan's pistol was an indication to Makal that they had defanged the lethal hunter, and Makal saw Gogin's shots bounce an abandoned light around before the destroyed mechanism toppled to the floor.

Makal spun behind the cover of a low chunk of wall. No follow-up shots from his adversary filled the air, which meant that the interloper hadn't much ammo to spare. Meanwhile, Gogin reloaded his rifle and continued his watch over the blackened cavern that was the remains of the house.

Makal grinned and squinted into the darkness. "You're surrounded and you don't have enough firepower to take either of us down. Why not just give up?"

"Not my style," Mack Bolan answered. His voice seemed to come from everywhere at once.

Yuli Makal somersaulted out of the way as the Executioner dropped to the floor. Had the Jandarma captain stayed put, Bolan could have shattered bones with the weight of his leap. Instead, Makal raised his CZ-75 at the big black shadow. Before the muzzle could lock on target, a boot crashed into Makal's wrist and knocked his aim off.

Bolan lunged in close, avoiding a burst of rifle fire from Gogin. Makal twisted under the Executioner's weight and he hammered the slide of the Czech pistol hard into his opponent's ribs.

The big American snaked an arm around Makal's neck and clamped his other hand on the wrist that held the Walther P-38. With a surge, Bolan levered Makal across his hip and ground him into the floor.

Gogin held his fire. Makal figured it was uncertainty, whether to cut loose and destroy the attacker and possibly kill his friend and partner in crime. Makal was certain Gogin, for all his misgivings about being an exile from Van, wouldn't turn his back on the Jandarma captain.

Makal snapped his forehead into Bolan's gut, then dug his shoulder in, lifting the big man with a surge of maniacal strength.

The Executioner suddenly lashed his legs around Makal's chest and pinned him in place. A wicked elbow strike left the Turkish captain's left arm numb, and the two men tumbled wildly into a brick wall. Earthquake-loosened mortar gave way and their combined, fighting mass plowed through, rubble bouncing off both men.

Makal squirmed to freedom, getting out of Bolan's leg scissors. He tried to bring his pistol into play again, but his adversary kneed his forearm and the shot cracked wildly into the darkness. Instead, the Turk rolled onto his back. He was disarmed now, except for the third Walther P-38 that he'd tucked into his waistband.

Gunfire pierced the shadows, and that forced Bolan and Makal to separate, bullets sparking on the ground between them.

"Gogin! What's going on?" Makal snapped.

Another burst cut through the darkness, the remnants of the weakened wall deflecting certain death for Makal.

"I'm cutting my losses! You see, you let an undercover operation go rotten. I put you in the ground, and I take out my remaining witness, a man known to have murdered at least four Jandarma troopers," Gogin explained.

The Executioner whipped out his Walther at the same time Makal did. The two men froze, guns in hand.

"Your friend switched sides," Bolan told him.

Makal had his handgun at a low ready, looking back toward the alley, then to the wraith in black. He sneered. "He's not my friend anymore."

"So do we kill each other or him?" Bolan asked.

Makal looked around the room they'd crashed into. There weren't many options for them. At point-blank range, the Jandarma enforcer and the Executioner would cut each other down. Even if Bolan had the first shot, the puny .380 wouldn't kill Makal instantly.

"Stand off," Makal mused.

Another rattle of rifle fire cut into the darkness, and the two combatants huddled deeper behind cover. Bricks toppled from the weakened wall, knocked aside by high-powered bullets.

In a few moments, there wouldn't even be the wreckage of the wall to protect them.

Something bounced in the darkness, and Makal and Bolan dived for a window at the same time.

Their combined weight destroyed the glass and wooden framework, bodies sailing through the hole seconds before a grenade detonated. Makal rolled to one side and swung the frame of his Walther at Bolan's face.

The Executioner blocked with his forearm and speared his own gun toward the Turk's guts. Makal dodged by slithering in close and used his elbow as a hammer to whack Bolan in the chest. That knocked the Walther off target. A single .380 slug barked and rocketed into the distance. Makal went for the head butt again, but Bolan twisted and caught the clubbing skull on his shoulder.

With a twist, Bolan hammered Makal's own gun hard into the Turk's face, steel ripping flesh and cracking the bone around his right eye. Pain exploded in the Jandarma captain's skull, but he held Bolan's gun hand in a powerful arm lock. Even stunned, the Turk pivoted on his heel and applied agonizing pressure to the Executioner's wrist.

Bolan swung his left fist toward Makal's throat, going for a larynx-crushing blow, but Makal took the hit on his chin. The Turk still saw flashing lights, but his windpipe hadn't collapsed and he could still breathe. If he had to take nourishment through a straw, it was no big deal to Makal. The Turk's P-38 struggled to get in line with Bolan's body. A 9 mm bullet cracked out of the muzzle, and Bolan jerked.

Makal grinned. It was payback for the flash-bang grenade that the Executioner had used on him before. The Turk pistoned his knee to catch Bolan in the crotch, but he struck only the thick muscle of Bolan's thigh.

The Executioner surged, hurling Makal down the gangway, finally breaking the Turk's armlock on him, but at the cost of the Walther. Bolan had pulled his knife and lunged in for the kill when a shape appeared at the far end of the walkway. The warrior ducked back through the window as automatic weapon fire sliced through the shadows.

Makal let loose a convincing gurgle and lay still, sliding to the floor of the gangway, behind the cover of an overturned drum.

The Jandarma captain, bruised and stunned, but untouched by enemy bullets, held his breath and waited for Gogin to shift his interest to the other man.

When he heard the G-3 rattle again, aimed at another target, Makal sprung to his feet and rushed toward the street.

A truck sat in front of the half-collapsed building, and Makal staggered toward it. When he found the keys still in the engine, and the satellite phone on the passenger seat, he said a silent thank-you to Inspector Brandon Stone, turned off the phone and drove away.

MACK BOLAN RACED THROUGH the shattered building as Gogin's rifle cracked, trying to track his movements. Pushed to his limits, the Executioner hadn't been able to defeat Makal, though the other Jandarma enforcer hadn't exactly given Bolan enough breathing room to take him down. If Bolan was lucky, Makal had stopped a burst of automatic fire in the gangway, but then, if Bolan had luck with him, he wouldn't have been caught in the middle of a civil war *and* an earthquake.

Bolan wasn't going to waste more brainpower on lamenting his run of ill fortune. Instead, he leaped over the crater left by Gogin's grenade and cut toward the opening. More 7.62 mm bullets chopped through rubble and inky blackness, seeking his flesh. The soldier had his knife, but Gogin was outside the range of his knife-throwing skills. He didn't want to throw away his only ready weapon on an effort that would result in a wound. He sheathed the blade and scrambled on all fours around the mountain of broken rubble that he'd crashed into.

The RPK was still available, on the floor somewhere.

It wasn't in the Executioner's spirit to quit, and he somersaulted around the corner of a flat slope of flooring and saw the wooden stock of the RPK glisten in moonlight from the hole in the wall.

"Stone!" Gogin shouted as he fumbled another magazine into his rifle.

Bolan sprung at the RPK and scooped it off the floor. The front sight snagged on a pile of bricks and nearly tore the light machine gun out of his grasp as he charged for cover. Gogin saw the movement and cut loose with his G-3, full-auto thunder splitting the night.

The Executioner crashed onto his shoulder, wrenched the RPK out of the pile and triggered it. Gogin's slugs rippled through the darkness, two slicing across his bicep, drawing blood and injecting molten pain into Bolan. But the light machine gun exploded into action, and the Turk screamed in horror as bullets shredded his thighs and pelvis.

Gogin toppled to the ground.

With a sigh, Bolan slung the RPK across his good shoulder, hurried to Gogin and took his handgun and spare ammo. He stuffed the pistol in his belt, then took the dead man's G-3 rifle for some extra firepower. Bolan had ammunition for the USP rifle, so it wouldn't be a wasted effort. He refreshed his depleted G-3 supplies from Gogin's, then finally pulled a roll of duct tape from his harness and took care of the gunshot wounds to his arm. He'd been grazed, but the shots hurt, and they bled. With a strip of torn cloth as a compress, and the duct tape holding the improvised bandage in place, Bolan figured his arm would last another night before he could get to medical assistance.

The Executioner stepped out into the street, bristling with weaponry, his body a road map of bruises, cuts and new gunshot wounds. When he reached the spot where he'd parked the pickup truck, it was gone.

Makal had escaped.

Bolan returned to Makal's VW, but stopped off to search Gogin's body.

The dead man's cell phone was soaked with blood, but it still worked.

He had calls to make, and doomsday numbers still rained out of control.

CATHERINE ABOOD HAD TO TURN over the Walther P-38 to Major Omar Baydur, but Lem Sengor stood by her side, keeping watch over her as medics looked her over. She hated being unarmed. There were just too many things she'd seen in Turkey for her to ever want to be in this country again with anything less than an AK-47 locked in her fists.

It hurt like hell when the medics reset her broken jaw and taped her up. Until they could get her to a hospital, which was unlikely in the wake of the earthquake, tape and bandages would have to keep her mandible immobilized. Painkillers ran through her system, and saline solution replaced the blood she'd lost from her abuse at the hands of Boz Arcuri. The addition of a glucose solution fed nourishment into her veins, and she was glad for that. Chewing would not be on her list of favorite activities for the next few months.

Sengor smiled at her and gave her hand a squeeze. "You'll be all right."

Abood nodded slowly. The movement didn't hurt as much as it used to. Still, a medic affixed a foam collar around her neck.

"Don't move your head, or your jaw will never heal," the medic told her in Turkish.

Abood rolled her eyes. "Yes, sir…" she murmured through barely moving lips.

"And no talking," the medic admonished.

Abood sighed.

"He's just doing his job," Sengor explained.

Abood only glared at the medic. Sengor was able to read her thoughts and he grinned at her reaction.

Abood leaned back and let out a low groan. Being denied the ability to speak or even express herself nonverbally with head movements, she might as well have been locked in a prison cell. Plus she'd have trouble typing and her left-hand penmanship was hideous.

The medics left Abood alone, and Sengor snaked an object from under his jacket.

"Your Beretta. I found it. Arcuri left it behind in the office," Sengor explained.

Abood smiled weakly, then took the gun and tucked it into her waistband.

"I figured that would make you happy," the Jandarma man said. "It's a nice pistol."

Abood gauged how she could respond to Sengor, but gave up and sighed. "Yeah."

"What did the doctor say about talking?"

Abood rolled her eyes again and glared at the Turk with the frosted-blond hair.

Something caught her attention over Sengor's shoulder, and her eyes narrowed.

Sengor turned to see where she was looking. "What's wrong?"

Abood struggled to her feet. The bags of saline, glucose and antibiotics crinkled where they'd been secured to her biceps by a length of rubber tubing. She slid her hand under her blouse, resting her fingers on the grip of her Beretta.

Through the haze of painkillers, she finally recognized

what had kicked her survival instincts into gear. Boz Arcuri stood, dressed in a soldier's uniform. There was no doubt that he had seen them, but surrounded by medics and Jandarma officers, Arcuri had other priorities. She wondered what, though. "Arcuri."

Sengor's phone rang, and he plucked it from his pocket. "Lem."

Abood froze and glanced at the Turk.

"Makal got away," Sengor relayed. "And we just spotted Arcuri."

Abood stepped away from Sengor, weaving through the ranks of Turkish soldiers. They were busy loading medical supplies into trucks and helicopters.

Omar Baydur stood off to one side, by his helicopter, talking on his own communicator. Abood wanted to shout at the top of her lungs. Arcuri, the insane maniac who had murdered hundreds of people the day before, was walking among them, unnoticed. She glanced to Sengor who jogged up to her side.

When she looked back, Arcuri was gone.

"Lost him?" Sengor asked.

Abood's lips tightened. She continued to look.

"We'll split up," Sengor promised her. "But don't pull your gun. Baydur is still fidgety about your involvement in the deaths of Makal's men."

Abood could only glare menacingly. The Jandarma man took the hint and took off through the crowd.

Catherine Abood let her left hand dangle down freely as she searched for the Kurdish bomber.

She hoped that she could find the maniac in time to prevent any more deaths.

Well, almost any more deaths.

The reporter intended to write Boz Arcuri's obituary, preferably in lead and fire.

Stony Man Farm, Virginia

"WE'VE GOT MAKAL on the screen now," Barbara Price explained. "The GPS in your satellite phone is tracking him easily."

"I'm just not closing in on him," Bolan noted. "Makal knows this city a lot better. I'm running into broken roads and collapsed buildings, and he's just putting more distance between us."

"I could call in some backup," Price offered.

"And risk the chance that we might actually tip off his friends in the Jandarma?" Bolan asked. "No, I'm going to have to take him down alone."

"Makal's making a call," Wethers announced. "Putting it on the screen."

Price looked up to the screen and saw the voice analysis, green spikes of lines forming words in a language she didn't know.

Kurtzman struggled to get the voice-recognition digital translation software working. It wasn't perfected software, and for a few moments, the captions under the line of Makal's voice were unintelligible gibberish.

"Crap," Kurtzman growled. "Turkish slang. Makal's not going to make this easy for us. The translation filter is just spewing out gobbledygook."

Price sighed. "And the other end?"

Wethers worked frantically. "Not getting anything."

"I've got activity on a landline," Tokaido responded. "Not far from the sat phone's GPS coordinates. Tapping it."

"Calling in some more backup," Bolan surmised. "See if that's who Makal is calling."

"We've got dialogue matching our digital recording," Tokaido announced. "Makal just called a restaurant."

"He sure as hell isn't making dinner reservations," Bolan said. "Anything, Aaron?"

"Just that whoever Makal is talking to offered a dozen gunmen to him," Kurtzman relayed. "You've still got a fight ahead of you. I wonder who he's tapped into."

"Offhand, I'd bet it's the creeps Makal intended to sell his share of the medical supplies to," Bolan guessed. "He might be selling them the story about how I rained on their parade."

"You've got the directions?" Price asked, continuing to supply the Executioner with information. "There's an unblocked intersection at your next turn."

"Got it," Bolan stated.

"Keep going for a mile and a half and you'll be there," Price announced. "Makal pulled into the parking lot."

"Aaron, get on the line to Baydur again," Bolan ordered. "Say that you picked up a transmission from Boz Arcuri in the area. Get the Jandarma on alert. Sengor told me that Cat spotted him blending in with the forces recovering the relief supplies."

"I'm still watching the area," Carmen Delahunt said. "Abood's making a beeline for whoever she just spotted."

"Striker?" Price asked.

"Going to work," Bolan replied. "I'll talk to you later."

The phone line went dead, and a blanket of tense silence hung in the Stony Man computer room.

Within the next few minutes, the final bloody battle of Van would be waged, and the cyberteam had front-row seats.

The sense of dread was thick enough to cut with a knife.

22

Boz Arcuri moved up against the side of the Black Hawk helicopter and pressed a small cake of plastic explosives in its doorway. The blast wouldn't knock the aircraft out of the sky. He didn't have enough C-4 for that task, but the blast would certainly kill crew members, and the resultant turbulence could force the Black Hawk to crash.

One less shipment of supplies to keep the undeserving citizens of Van alive. More corpses to serve as Arcuri's harbingers into death.

He'd sabotaged three helicopters already, moving unnoticed among the troops, his swarthy features matching theirs, his military uniform taken from a Jandarma trooper. The uniform's previous owner was dead, neck broken, corpse stuffed nearly naked under a set of steps.

Arcuri grinned.

By the time they'd figured out what Arcuri had done, even if they gunned him down, thousands more would die. All due to his interference.

Arcuri was going to sweep the city of Van clean, its useless eaters left to die in pain and suffering, their only hopes blown out of the sky.

And Arcuri would march into hell, a champion of death and revenge.

All for Recep.

The only good human being in the rotten city, murdered by the conniving interference of a nosy bitch. "This is for you, cousin."

He heard someone clear their throat behind him. Arcuri turned, and saw Catherine Abood standing there, her face framed in bandages and a foam collar. She looked almost comical, wrapped up like a mummy, but there was no humor in her gaze, nor was there anything funny about the squares of explosives poking out of her sling.

"Forgot something," Abood grumbled.

Arcuri looked around and saw Lem Sengor approaching from another angle.

Further racket erupted, and Arcuri spotted movement by Major Omar Baydur's helicopter. The Jandarma commander and a group of men raced toward him. Arcuri looked at the explosives he'd pressed into the Black Hawk's door frame, then back at Abood.

She dropped the radio detonators on the ground. The cakes she had rested in her sling were inert, lifeless.

Abood smirked. "Misery...company."

Arcuri reached for his radio detonator, but the reporter pulled out her Beretta in a lightning-fast movement. The Kurd howled as a 9 mm slug tore through his forearm, killing all sensation to his hand. The thumb stud didn't trip.

Abood fired two more shots, both slugs spearing into Arcuri's groin. Agony flooded through the Kurd as his radio detonator tumbled from insensate fingers. He coughed, burning with pain that boiled up from his smashed pelvis.

Shouting filled the air, and Jandarma troops drew their weapons, taking aim at the woman who had gunned down one of their own. Lem Sengor leaped out of nowhere and yanked Abood to the ground, the Beretta clattering on the concrete.

The roar of blood rushing in Arcuri's ears, spurred on by pain, kept him from hearing what Sengor said as he pressed the American reporter against the concrete. Major Baydur rushed up and placed himself between Abood and the rest of his enforcers.

Arcuri looked at the slick, silver-finished little Beretta she'd gunned him down with. He reached out, fingers digging into the concrete. He tried to pull himself closer to the gun with his good hand. His fingertips had just brushed the soft rubber grips, when a boot crashed down, snapping his forearm bones.

He glanced up at Baydur, standing on his mangled arm, the barrel of a handgun leveled at a spot between Arcuri's eyes.

"You won't kill me, you weakling," Arcuri said, cackling. "You're here to prevent men like Makal from executing Kurds!"

Baydur looked at Sengor and Abood. The frosted-blond Jandarma man cradled the wounded reporter. He scanned the rest of his men, their fingers poised over triggers. Hearts hammered as they waited for the response from their commander.

Beneath the major's boot, Boz Arcuri laughed, the last shreds of sanity snapping. Baydur stepped harder on the broken bones, and the laugh dissolved into a howl that stopped only when Baydur smashed the muzzle of his handgun between the maniacal Kurd's teeth.

"I came here to keep Makal from executing and torturing the innocent," Baydur said loud enough to be heard. "You are not innocent."

Boz Arcuri's head exploded as Baydur's bullet tore through it.

YULI MAKAL LIMPED as he got out of the pickup truck. He had no doubt that the avenging wraith's allies were listening on the phone, and within moments, Stone would be tearing down behind him. There was a pistol in the glove compartment, and Makal stuffed that into his waistband, as backup to the partially spent Walther.

The restaurant was full of armed Kurdish People's Party veterans. A dozen men who had bloodied themselves in previous campaigns of insurgency against the Turkish regime. It was the only thing that Makal knew that he could put between himself and the furious avenger on his heels. Makal glanced back, then dialed Gogin's phone.

"I'm coming, Makal," Stone said.

"Good job surviving," Makal congratulated him. "You want a piece of me, you probably know where I am."

Headlights flared in the distance. "Yes, I do."

Makal chuckled and he looked back at the restaurant. Gunmen came out the doors, their rifles leveled at the pickup truck. The Jandarma captain tumbled into the bed of the truck, escaping their notice for a moment. It wouldn't last long.

"Then come get me," Makal grated. He hung up the phone and curled behind the concealing walls of the truck bed.

"Where's that bastard, Makal?" one of the PKK thugs asked.

"Check the truck. See if he at least brought us the morphine," another said.

"If he didn't bring it, I'm going to rip his balls off personally and cram them down his throat," a third of the thugs complained.

"Get in line," the first speaker responded.

Makal slithered under a concealing tarpaulin. From the smell of gun oil, the tarp had to have been covering a small arsenal. Then again, he thought, this truck had to have been used by Kagan Trug's men to bring the extra gunners to the battle at the warehouse.

The tarp would give Makal another few moments of repose, enough to give Stone the chance to swing by and use up whatever hellish vengeance against the Kurdish gangsters. And when they were dead, Yuli Makal would have his final say.

A death's-head grin planted itself on the renegade's face as he clutched his handgun tightly.

MACK BOLAN RESTED the RPK on the dashboard of the VW as he spotted the gunmen heading out to Makal's pickup truck. He hadn't checked the bed of the vehicle to see if there had been any other heavy weapons in the back, but if there were, the local thugs were probably in a hurry to get them.

Bolan hit the brakes ten yards from the pickup truck as the riflemen were about to get into the truck bed.

"Drop your weapons!" Bolan announced. He didn't know who these men were, but from the looks of their AK-47s, they certainly weren't part of a Boy Scout troop.

One of the gunners snapped to attention and opened fire, haste throwing the first rounds from his rifle into the VW's engine and killing it. Bolan put a burst of RPK thunder through the rifleman's heart, and his corpse rocketed away from the pickup truck.

The other riflemen, speaking rapidly in Kurdish, opened fire, and the Executioner was no longer worried about burning down possible soldiers on the same side. Makal had come to these men for shelter and backup. Their willingness to kill was simply the final nail in their coffins, and Bolan tore into them.

The ammo drum clanked empty, and rather than fuss with reloading, the Executioner ducked behind the wheel well of the shot-up VW. AK-47s chattered angrily at him, but Bolan snaked his HK G-3 around and flicked the selector to full-auto. He ducked underneath the vehicle and saw several sets of feet charging toward him.

Bolan cut loose, high-powered rifle rounds slicing though

shins and ankles. The raw power of the 7.62 mm NATO slugs severed feet and lower legs with one solid hit, and wounded Kurds toppled to the ground. When the G-3 cycled dry, the Executioner plucked a grenade from his harness, armed the bomb and lobbed it over the top of the vehicle. He scrambled behind the shelter of the VW's tire and axle.

Instants later, a blossom of fire and shrapnel cut through enemy bodies. The fallen wounded and those still running were slammed into oblivion by a sheet of flaming hot metal. The VW's tires absorbed superheated wire, and they hissed rabidly, air disgorging from their pierced shells. Bolan peered across the hood as he slammed another magazine home, and saw that everyone between the VW and the pickup were on the ground, covered with gory wounds. Some of the men still moved and twitched, and Bolan punched single shots into them as he broke cover.

The Executioner skidded to a halt next to the driver's-side door of the pickup. It had been left open, and that set the warrior's instincts on fire. Something was wrong with this picture.

Bolan leaned in and saw that the keys were gone, but he knew that he could easily hot-wire the pickup. He glanced into the bed and saw a tangled tarp wadded up in the corner. He was about to reach down to see if Kagan Trug had left any hardware behind when the second wave of gunners cut loose on the truck.

The Executioner swung around to the front of the vehicle and hammered off a burst that caught a Kurdish thug at waist level. Heavy-caliber bullets cut the man in two and he hit the ground, leaving a streak of blood and body parts behind him. Bolan lifted his aim and blew the head off a second of the terrorists, chunks of skull and brain hurtling apart in a cloud of devastation.

Of the "dozen boys" that Kurtzman quoted, Bolan could

account for seven of them. The other five had to have retreated into the restaurant in the face of a blisteringly brutal resistance.

The Executioner jogged toward the restaurant entrance. With his hurt right arm, he grabbed a grenade off his harness and armed it. Using the barrel of the G-3, he smashed a hole in a window and hurled the minibomb through the broken glass. A quick step took him to the cover of the brick wall.

One rifleman dived out of the window in an effort to escape the explosion that followed an instant later. The grenade detonated, and another body came through the glass, flopped half over the window frame.

The Kurd who had dived for cover scrambled to his feet, but Bolan triggered his rifle and powerful slugs hammered the dying terrorist, kicking him over messily. Shattered ribs poked through his lifeless chest, and sightless eyes stared glassily into the night sky.

Bolan turned and kicked open the restaurant door, staying behind the cover of the doorjamb. Gunshots rang out inside, peppering the broken door. From their sound and speed, they were only handguns, which meant that the Executioner had cut the enemy's power to resist significantly. He reloaded and kicked the door again, firing at knee height with the mighty USP. Bullets leaped through space and tore through the flimsy wood and glass of the register's counter. The pistol-packing PKK goon who had taken cover there convulsed violently as the high-powered projectiles chewed into him.

Another handgun barked in the depths of the restaurant. Bolan backed out and went to the shattered window. The shades had been blown to shreds, and the Executioner spotted the last Kurdish gunman behind the cover of a table.

Bolan held down the trigger on the G-3 and obliterated the last of Makal's defenders with the last of his magazine. He fished out another magazine to feed the hungry rifle.

The pickup truck shifted as something moved in its bed, and before Bolan could roll to cover, a bullet punched through the tarp and stabbed into his right arm. It took everything in the warrior's power not to clamp his good hand over his injured arm and claw for the P-38 that he'd taken from Gogin.

Makal hurled off his tarpaulin and pulled the trigger on his Walther again. This time, though, the handgun didn't speak. With a curse, the Jandarma man hurled the jammed pistol aside and he reached for the PPK he'd jammed in his waistband.

"You're dead, Stone!" Makal shouted as he leaped out of the truck bed, putting the vehicle's frame between himself and Bolan's return fire.

Bolan scrambled into the entrance of the restaurant, crawling ahead of bullets snapping at his heels. On the other side of the doorway, he leaned out and triggered his pistol twice more at Makal.

The Jandarma captain raced out of the arc of fire provided by the entrance, and Bolan knew that the renegade was going for one of the Kurds' rifles. It was a brilliant strategy, letting others distract and exhaust Bolan's weaponry and strength. The P-38 had four more shots in it.

With every ounce of strength, Bolan pushed to his feet and saw Makal stoop for a dead man's rifle.

The Executioner triggered a shot, but Makal was moving too quickly. He hit the Turk, but it was only a glancing shot.

Makal stumbled and dived under the cover of the window. Bolan lurched forward when the AK-47 popped over the bottom sill and chattered on full-auto. He took cover in a booth, the heavy wood and foam absorbing slugs.

Bolan took a deep breath and let the Walther clatter to the floor. He poked his bloody right arm out, a waterfall of crimson running down his fingers.

Glass flew as Makal cleared jagged shards out of his path.

Bolan couldn't see, but he heard the crunch of glass as Makal crawled in the window. The AK-47 crashed to the floor, and he heard the clatter of a handgun being picked up.

Even as he listened, Bolan snaked his left hand to his knife sheath and drew it. He knew it would take perfect timing, but if he got it right...

Makal racked the slide on the dead Kurd's pistol, then fed it a magazine. It was noisy work, but the Jandarma captain was taking his time, counting on Bolan to bleed to death. The murderer probably figured that Bolan was only playing possum, and he wanted to be good and ready for any surprise that the Executioner had in mind.

The combat knife was clenched in Bolan's left hand. Blood continued to drip off his fingertips.

He was losing blood quickly, so Makal's tactics had merit. Bolan's legs tensed as he heard Makal's footsteps approaching.

"Don't worry, Stone. I'll make sure the bad guys keep dying for you," the Turk promised as he stepped into the open, handgun leveled at the wounded warrior.

The Executioner sprang like a trap, his full weight rocketing into Makal's midsection before the killer could pull the trigger. Their bodies hurtled across the restaurant, smashing through two tables.

Makal's handgun tumbled from his grip and he flopped to the floor.

The Turk tried to sit up, but something burned, hard and ugly in his gut.

Makal looked down and saw the bloody handle of Bolan's combat knife jutting from his belly. Cold, wet darkness flooded up from his abdomen and trickled from his mouth as he looked at the Executioner.

"You only have to worry about yourself," the Executioner said. He bent and picked up the handgun and aimed at a spot between Makal's eyes, but a bullet wasn't needed.

The corrupt Jandarma commander was already dead.

Bolan stuffed the pistol into his waistband, then took his satellite phone from Makal's corpse.

"Striker?" he heard Barbara Price answer.

"Yeah," Bolan told her. "What's the word on Arcuri?"

"Baydur killed him," Price responded. "Abood and Sengor are all right."

Bolan smiled. "Call Baydur back and tell him I've been shot. I'll need some medical assistance."

"We're sending him," Price promised. "You'll be okay?"

Bolan stepped into the parking lot. Street lamps flickered to life, and various buildings started lighting up. The city of Van was returning to life slowly but surely. It would take a lot of rebuilding, but the Turks and Kurds, if they worked together, could get the metropolis back in business in time. With Makal, Trug and Arcuri gone, Bolan knew peaceful cooperation would go a lot more smoothly.

"You'll be okay, Striker?" Price asked.

A helicopter circled to land and bring the warrior medical assistance. "Soon enough," Mack Bolan answered.

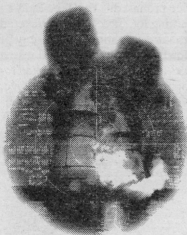

James Axler
Outlanders

**An ancient Chinese emperor
stakes his own dark claim to Earth…**

HYDRA'S RING

A sacred pyramid in China is invaded by what appears to be a ruthless
Tong crime lord and his army. But a stunning artifact and a desperate
summons for the Cerberus exiles put the true nature of the looming battle
into horrifying perspective. Kane and his rebels must confront a four-
thousand-year-old emperor, an evil entity as powerful as any nightmare
now threatening humankind's future….

Available November 2006 wherever you buy books.